MURDER IN MOSCOW

A FIONA FIGG & KITTY LANE MYSTERY

KELLY OLIVER

Boldwood

First published in Great Britain in 2024 by Boldwood Books Ltd.

Copyright © Kelly Oliver, 2024

Cover Design by Alexandra Allden

Cover Images: Shutterstock and Getty

Every effort has been made to obtain the necessary permissions with reference to copyright material, both illustrative and quoted. We apologise for any omissions in this respect and will be pleased to make the appropriate acknowledgements in any future edition.

A CIP catalogue record for this book is available from the British Library.

Paperback ISBN 978-1-80483-200-4

Large Print ISBN 978-1-80483-201-1

Hardback ISBN 978-1-80483-199-1

Ebook ISBN 978-1-80483-202-8

Kindle ISBN 978-1-80483-203-5

Audio CD ISBN 978-1-80483-194-6

MP3 CD ISBN 978-1-80483-195-3

Digital audio download ISBN 978-1-80483-197-7

Boldwood Books Ltd
23 Bowerdean Street
London SW6 3TN
www.boldwoodbooks.com

KITTY'S PROLOGUE
27 FEBRUARY 1918, 10 A.M.

Kitty Lane reached across the table for the letter she'd found on Aunt Fiona's nightstand. She uncrumpled it and reread the last line:

Fiona, ma chérie, ... join me at Metropol Hotel, Suite 315. I offer you only the world.

What an arrogant arse. Snorting, she dropped the letter next to the gun she'd found in the nightstand. Aunt Fiona's little pearl-handled number that she always bragged she'd got off the famous French spy, Mata Hari. Kitty resisted the urge to kick something. It wasn't her place, after all. She glanced around. In Aunt Fiona's kitchen, everything was as immaculate as pent-up passion. No red, or proper pink, not forest-green or even lime. Instead, pale colors, washed out and muted. From the scrubbed enameled stove and the dust-free paraffin lamps to the pale-pink ceiling and mint-green wallpaper, the cramped space exuded repression. Too bad Aunt Fiona had suddenly decided to follow her heart. Never a good idea.

Kitty stared down at the letter. *What is the body but the vanity of the soul?* Talk about vanity. She crumpled up the letter again, tossed it onto the kitchen table, and then stood up with such force, she nearly knocked over the chair. Pacing the length of the small kitchen, she debated her options. Hot on her heels, the little dog smacked into her foot. "Sorry, Poppy." The Pekingese had been her constant companion since she'd returned from France four months ago, just before her first assignment partnered with Fiona Figg. She adjusted the pink bow on the dog's topknot. It matched the one she wore in her own hair. Although Poppy's butterscotch hair was a few shades darker than Kitty's, they both looked fabulous in pink.

She turned around and stopped in front of the telephone box on the wall. She plucked a piece of paper from behind the box. It read *Archie* and had a telephone number. How sweet. Aunt Fiona had Archie's number tucked between the phone box and the wall. Lieutenant Archie Somersby, Aunt Fiona's fiancé. Not anymore. Not after Aunt Fiona's latest stunt. Should she call him and tell him? Tell him what? That Fiona had run after another man? Aunt Fiona should have stuck with the flyboy. At least he was on their side. No. Fiona had to run after that scoundrel Fritz Duquesne, alias Fredrick Fredricks, a known assassin and German spy who called himself "The Panther." Fiona had no idea what she was up against. She didn't even know his real name was Fritz Duquesne. It was classified. Beyond her clearance level. And bound to get her killed.

Kitty bent down and scooped up her little furry friend and grabbed Mata Hari's gun. "Time to face the music, Poppy-poo." Tucking the squirming pup under her arm, she marched out of the kitchen, back through the flat—stopping only to pluck one of Aunt Fiona's wigs from its stand on the dressing table—and then slammed the door on the way out.

1

COUNTESS BRASOVA

A heart at war with itself. For the dozenth time, I repeated the phrase from the letter he'd left in my flat. I shouldn't have followed the bounder from London to Moscow. What was I thinking? Was I completely daft? Concentrating on inhaling and exhaling, I squeezed my eyes shut. At twenty-five, I should have known better. Trailing Fredrick Fredricks for the War Office was one thing, but accepting his invitation for personal—ahem, romantic —reasons was quite another. Even if I didn't end up with a broken skull, I'd end up with a broken heart.

Fredrick Fredricks. South African huntsman, sometimes journalist, and very clever German spy—an enemy spy—who repeatedly claimed he wanted to stop the war. With his dancing eyes and mischievous smile, he was also too darn charming for his own good—or mine. How could I let myself fall for such a cad? I'd really done it this time.

I took another turn around the hotel suite. Stopping at the desk, I picked up one of the hotel postcards. *The Metropol Hotel, Russia's finest. Sigh.* Like most buildings in Moscow, the hotel had open wounds that would take years to heal. Russia's finest was riddled with bullet holes and littered with bits of plaster. Many of the windows were broken and boarded, and armed guards patrolled every floor. My canopy bed had a bullet embedded in its frame, and the gold satin chairs and matching divan sat proudly in the midst of plaster dust. Like a wounded war hero, beneath its superficial scars the hotel exuded splendor, weary but beyond pity.

Damaged by bombing, the restaurant was closed, but food and wine were served in the private rooms. I felt like a princess locked in a gilded tower waiting for her prince to return. I strolled to the window—the only one not boarded up. Through cracked glass, I stared out as if I might spot him passing by on the street below. Instead, wearing shabby coats and hats, dozens of women banged on pots and shouted in Russian, their breath freezing into frosty clouds. I guessed they were protesting about the lack of food. I shivered just watching them out there in the cold. Across Europe and beyond, the war had taken its toll on everyone. Even kings were tightening their belts. Back home, King George V showed off his ration card, hoping he didn't end up like his cousin, Tsar Nicholas II, who'd been exiled to Siberia. Some of the codebreakers in the War Office worried what was happening in Russia was a preview of things to come for England. *I sincerely hope not.*

In the two days since I arrived, it had become obvious this country was being torn apart by wars both abroad and at home. Things were bad back in England, but this was worse. Much worse. Every building within a mile was pocked with artillery shells. Not from the Germans but from civil war. A country turned against itself. And yet, judging by the sounds of music and laughter coming from neighboring rooms at all hours, guests at the Metropol Hotel celebrated like there was no tomorrow.

I dropped the postcard into my skirt pocket and then plopped down into a posh chair and flipped through an issue of *Moscow Magazine*. The centerpiece was an exhibit by a Russian painter named Wassily Kandinsky, who had recently been appointed head of the arts division of the People's Commissariat for Enlightenment. I studied the brightly colored images. A world in motion, a rolling and roiling world of color and shapes, a world turned inside out. Much like the broken city outside my window, only more vibrant. A phrase caught my eye: *like a mad tuba*. He called the Moscow sunset a mad tuba vibrating in the soul. My heart felt like a mad tuba. I tossed the magazine onto the coffee table and then resumed my pacing.

I'd been here two days and no sign of Fredricks—except fresh flowers delivered daily. He was nothing if not extravagant. While everyone else had to wait for a glimpse of wildflowers in spring and felt lucky to dine on leftover war bread, Fredricks secured roses and dined on strawberries and champagne. Upon my arrival, a small card attached to the first dozen red roses read only:

Back soon, ma chérie.

Back soon. Ha! *Back soon* was something you said when you ran down the street for a pint of milk or a bag of sugar, not when you disappeared into the murky political landscape of a war-torn country.

The cards that came with the flowers had an odd insignia, an oval with a sword cutting it in half and a big V in the center. Was it a clue to Fredricks's whereabouts? There had to be a clue somewhere in this suite. A clue as to why he was in Russia. A clue as to why he invited me here. Not just to Russia, or Moscow, or the Metropol Hotel, but to suite 315. I opened the closet again, as I'd done nearly every hour since I'd arrived. A woolen hunting jacket

hung over a white ruffled shirt. On the same hanger, completing
the ensemble, khaki jodhpurs peeked out below. Tall black boots
stood underneath, creating the uncanny sense of a headless
soldier standing at attention. I caressed the sleeve of the jacket,
glanced around the suite, and then leaned forward to smell the
collar. Sandalwood, mustache wax, and something else... something stalwart and dark. I slipped my hands into the jacket's pockets, closed my eyes, and imagined an embrace. *Fredricks, where are
you? Why aren't you here?*

Wait. *What's that?* My fingertip brushed against the point of
something. Something I must have missed the dozen other times
I'd slid my hands into his pockets. I pinched the small box
between my thumb and forefinger and withdrew it. A colorful
matchbox adorned with a growling tiger. I turned it over. On the
underside, in black pencil, were three cryptic lines:

03-03 B-L.
10-03 P-M.
??-?? WRD.

One of Fredricks's secret codes? Not a simple number to letter
transcription. 03-03. What was 03-03? I resumed pacing. It helped
me concentrate. Could it be a date—3 March? Four days from
now. *What happens on 3 March?* If it was a date, then the second
entry would be 10 March. Over one week later.

A rapping at the door interrupted my cogitations. "Fredricks?"
My breath caught. He was back. I stuffed the matchbox into my
skirt pocket and vowed to get the code out of him if I had to resort
to torture—or something more enjoyable. I smiled to myself. Not
that torturing Fredricks wouldn't be fun. Quickly, I went to the
dressing table and looked at myself in the mirror. I immediately
regretted it. My swollen eyes were as purple as two plums, my

cheeks as pasty as mealy pudding, and my lips dry and drawn. I patted my wig and adjusted my skirt. Sadly, no amount of patting or preening would make me pretty. Even before lost loves, sleepless nights, and war rations, I was no beauty.

I went to the door and stood there with my hand on the doorknob. I took a deep breath. Then another. Then another. Was I ready to face him? One more deep breath. Finally, I turned the knob and opened it.

My heart sank. Not Fredricks, but the aging porter. Trailing him was an attractive woman wearing feathers and furs. With her perfectly oval face, deep melancholy eyes, and long thin nose, she looked rather like a barn owl. Lips twitching, the porter introduced her as Countess Brasova. I peered out the door at her. Why in the world would a countess visit me? And what was proper etiquette when meeting Russian aristocrats? I extended my hand, thought better of it, and bobbed a curtsey. "How do you do?"

She gave me the weakest of smiles.

"I'm afraid there's been a mix-up and the countess needs your suite." The porter shifted from foot to foot. "I'll have to ask you to vacate within the hour." His white mustache twitched.

"You've got to be joking." I blinked at him. Vacate within the hour. "You're moving me to another suite?"

"No, ma'am." He grimaced. "We don't have any more habitable rooms." He stared down at his shoes. "I'm sorry."

I felt the blood drain from my face. He was throwing me out onto the street? "Where will I go?" I looked from the porter to the countess. Neither said a word. I squinted at the porter. "Has Mr. Fredricks checked in yet? Fredrick Fredricks?"

"No, ma'am." He shrugged. "No one by that name."

"But this suite belongs to him. He arranged for me to meet him here. He even put my name on the reservation. Could he have checked in under another name?" Fredricks often used aliases. "Over six feet tall, broad shoulders, long black hair and mustache..." Devilishly attractive and irresistibly charming. "Possibly wearing a slouch hat and jodhpurs, carrying a riding stick." I waved an imaginary stick. "Wears a gold ring with a panther insignia."

The porter and Countess Brasova exchanged glances. "Duke Zakrevsky," they said in unison. A Russian duke. What would the cad think of next? Duke Zakrevsky. That name was familiar.

Countess Brasova's eyes lit up. "You know the duke?" She stepped out from behind the porter, removed a gloved hand from her fur muff, and extended it to me. "I'm Natalia Romanov, but my friends call me Natasha."

"Romanov as in Tsar Nicholas?" My mouth fell open.

She put her hand on my arm as if we were best friends. "My husband Michael is his brother."

Golly. The Russian aristocrat was actually Russian royalty. Wait a minute. I seemed to remember something about the tsar's brother being exiled in disgrace for marrying a divorcee. As a divorcee myself, I sympathized. But not enough to accept eviction. I wasn't about to sleep on the street, not even for the tsar himself. "I really don't have anywhere else to go and I'm not about to—"

She squeezed my hand. "Of course, I wouldn't think of letting you give up your suite." She smiled at the porter. "Ivan, be a good boy and find me another room." With his white mustache and beard, Ivan was hardly a boy. "And send up some tea." She turned back to me. "And then you can tell me all about your friend Duke Zakrevsky."

Taking my arm, the countess led me back into my suite. *My suite.* She'd invited herself in for tea. *Sigh.* I let her lead me to the small sitting area near the boarded-up window. "How long have you known the duke?" Her accent gave her voice a purring quality, like a cat's before it pounced on an unsuspecting canary.

Apparently, I was the only one who *didn't* know "the duke."

The countess took a seat on the divan across from me. "Are the two of you... *close*?" The way she extended the word made it sound obscene.

"Umhmm." I nodded. After all, it was my proximity—or lack thereof—to the duke that had turned the countess from my heartless evictor into my bosom pal. The question was why. What was Fredricks up to now? "How do *you* know the duke?" I asked, relaxing back into the chair. Please, clue me in.

Sprawling across the divan, she crossed her long legs. "I was hoping you might introduce him to me," she said, chuckling. "I've heard so much about him... and about you, of course."

About me? Now I knew she was lying.

She waved a hand in front of her face like she'd smelled something bad. "You must know *Comrade* Lenin."

"The head of the Bolshevik government?" Why in the world would I know Mister, er, Comrade, Lenin?

"Are you friendly with Vladimir?" She tightened her thin lips, which accentuated her owl-like features.

Should I look for Fredricks in the Kremlin? I shook my head. How did he do it? Ingratiate himself to world leaders from that American president Teddy Roosevelt to the emperor of Austria. Men and women alike loved Fredricks—or the duke—or whatever other aliases he was using.

A soft knock at the door signaled the return of the porter with our tea. Scurrying around the sitting area, he sat the silver tea service on the low table and poured us both a cup. Alongside the teapot sat a plate of Russian tea biscuits. Obviously, Countess Brasova merited special treatment. My tea had never been accompanied by sweet biscuits. Nor had it been served in such an extravagant tea service with an ornate silver tray and teapot and delicate floral-patterned china.

"I was hoping the duke might put a word in for my husband." The countess straightened and took up her tea.

The duke. Duke Zakrevsky. Aha! I remembered. I'd seen that name on one of Fredricks's fake passports.

I gazed at her over the rim of my cup as I sipped. The Russians did make a fine strong cuppa. Very soothing. Especially accompanied by the fresh cream, no doubt due to the presence of the countess.

"The Cheka arrested him." A cloud passed over her breezy countenance.

I'd heard of the Cheka—the Bolshevik secret police.

"It's all a great mistake, of course." She sat her cup on its saucer. "I've appealed to Iron Victor. But he laughed in my face." Her cheeks reddened.

Iron Victor? Goodness.

"Victor Volodarsky. Head of the Cheka. Evil man." Jerking her head, she brushed a tear from her cheek. "Only Mr. Lenin can help us now, if your duke could put in a good word with him."

"Put in a good word for your husband?" I continued to peer over my teacup. "With Mister... er, Vladimir."

"They're together night and day, negotiating with those German *pridurki*." She picked imaginary lint from her muff.

I didn't know what *pridurki* meant, but I knew it wasn't good. Fredrick Fredricks and Vladimir Lenin together night and day negotiating with the Germans. Forget about *pridurki*. This was worse. Much worse. Russia had been an important ally. Now they were about to surrender to our enemy.

"I have half a mind to go to Lenin myself," she huffed. "How dare they arrest Michael." Her dark eyes flashed. "With his brother's abdication, he is the head of the royal family." She picked up her tea and stared down at it as if it might be poisoned. In view of the resentment toward the royal family, her fears might be justified.

"Do you know where these negotiations are taking place?" I tried to sound nonchalant.

"It's OB, top-secret." She leaned forward and lowered her voice. "But I have it on good authority they're in Brest-on-the-Bug."

"Brest-on-the-Bug," I repeated.

"Brest-Litovsk on the Bug River." She twisted around and pointed toward the window. "Southwest of here, near Warsaw. Now occupied by those German *pridurki*."

Fredricks was with Lenin at Bug River. My mind was awhirl. I pulled out my notebook and a pencil and jotted down an abbreviated version of the information.

Brest-Litovsk at the Bug River ala Countess Brasova.

B-L @ B-R ala C-B. Good heavens. B-L. That was the notation on Fredricks's matchbox. *03-03 B-L.* He was in B-L. What was happening in B-L on 3 March?

"I'm sorry to bring you into the middle of this." The countess's eyes were pleading. "But I'm desperate." She bit her lip. "I'm afraid of what they'll do to Michael. The Cheka are brutal."

I shuddered to think.

"I feel so helpless." When she slumped on the divan, her long limbs seemed to fold in on themselves. Her shoulders began to shake. Oh dear. Was she sobbing?

"There, there." I went over and sat next to her. "I'm certain the duke will help free your husband." I wasn't certain. In fact, I rather doubted that *the duke* would be inclined to help restore the monarchy if he was busy negotiating with the Germans. If I understood the situation correctly, Mr. Lenin and the Bolsheviks were decidedly anti-tsarist. To them, the royal family represented a threat. I wasn't quite sure about the Bolsheviks' stance on Germany. Politics was not my strong suit. Give me a complex filing system any day. Complicated politics gave me a headache. But I was certain of one thing. In the name of peace, Fredricks would do anything to ensure Germany's victory over Britain—an unfortunate sticking point in our relationship. Not that we *had* a relationship, mind you.

I withdrew a handkerchief from my skirt pocket and handed it to the countess. Sniffling, she took it. I put my arm around her trembling shoulders. "Countess, why don't you finish your tea?" I picked up her cup and saucer and held it out. "It will make you feel better." My grandmother always said everything was better with a nice cuppa. But my grandmother never had a run-in with the police, secret or otherwise.

Perhaps something stronger would be more appropriate. "Should I call for a brandy? Or a whiskey, perhaps?" I usually didn't go in for drinking, especially before noon, but the countess was melting into a messy puddle in my hotel suite. "To calm your nerves." I couldn't very well chuck her out, no matter how eager I was to find Fredricks and foil his plot, whatever it was.

Maybe if I found Fredricks and thwarted his plans, then I could redeem myself with the War Office. I cringed. No doubt I'd been sacked. And just when I was getting jolly good at espionage. What excuse could I give for waiting almost two weeks to report in? Kidnapped. I could say Fredricks had kidnapped me, and I didn't have a choice, and I would have called if only I could have. I wasn't following my heart but doing my duty. Would Captain Hall believe me? Disguises were one thing. Bald-faced lies were quite another.

"Yes, perhaps a brandy would be good." The countess's voice

was small. Her demeanor had totally transformed from the confident, entitled aristocrat she'd been when she arrived, to a bereft woman fighting for the man she loved. The war was the great leveler. I plucked a fancy biscuit from the plate. At least in some ways.

Thud. Thud. The porter's knock was harder than before. Perfect timing. I could order that restorative for the countess and then get rid of her. I patted her arm and then went to the door. When I opened it, a bearded man barged in. He looked menacing in his black leather jacket, tall black boots, and woolen mariner's cap. In the hall another man in uniform and armed with a bayonet stood at attention.

"Natalia Romanov." The bearded man barked out her name. "*Vy arestovany.*" He glanced at me. I didn't understand what he'd said, but I knew from his tone it wasn't good.

"Under arrest!" The countess jumped up. "But why?" She'd knocked her cup and saucer to the floor. At the sound of the breaking china, the armed guard dashed into the suite, bayonet aimed at me.

"*Vy oba.*" The leather-clad Cheka grabbed my arm. "*Vy arestovany.*"

"Both of us? But Miss Figg hasn't done anything." Arms akimbo, the countess stared them down as she spat something at them in Russian.

I yanked my arm away. "I'm a British citizen, a visitor from London."

"*Zalmochi.*" The copper shoved me toward the door.

I lost my footing and fell. I hit the floor with a thud.

"Don't tell her to shut up!" The countess ran to my side. She yelled something at them.

One of the Cheka pointed his bayonet at me.

"I twisted my ankle," I whined. Holding my ankle, I rolled around on the floor.

The countess kicked the Cheka in the shin. He grabbed her by the hair, and she screamed. Both guards were on her now. I took advantage of the distraction and slipped my notebook out of my pocket. Quickly, I scrawled "CHEKA" in big letters and then skated the notebook under the nearest piece of furniture. An armoire that stood next to the door. A big hand was around my upper arm. The Cheka yanked me to my feet. His partner seized the countess around the waist and dragged her from the suite. Struggling, she managed to knock his hat off. But that only made him angry. He threw her against the wall and then brought the butt of his rifle down on her head. She fell to the floor in a heap.

I gasped and my hand flew to my mouth. Good heavens. These Cheka *pridurki* were going to kill us.

Thwack. What felt like a horse's kick to the skull threw me to the ground. Holding my head in both hands, I moaned. My vision blurred. Then everything went black.

KITTY'S INTERLUDE
27 FEBRUARY, 2 P.M.

"Where is Miss Figg?" His lashes batting a mile a minute, Uncle Blinker tapped the pencil on his desk. Captain Blinker Hall was a small man sitting behind a big desk. What he lacked in stature, he made up for in forcefulness. Behind his gruff exterior, Kitty knew he had a soft heart. When she was thirteen, he'd rescued her from the streets of London and sent her to L'Espion espionage academy in France. He wasn't really her uncle. Neither was Fiona Figg her aunt. In France, she'd learned to call anyone older than herself—which meant over eighteen—"aunt" or "uncle." More than terms of deference, they were tools for disarming the enemy. And disarming the enemy was key to defeating them. Lesson number one of spy craft.

"Why hasn't she reported in?" He poked the air with the pencil and then went back to drumming.

Kitty settled into the plush chair across from the desk. Poppy sat at attention near her feet.

"She has a lead on Fredrick Fredricks."

Poppy barked. The pup wasn't a very good liar. To be fair, it wasn't exactly a lie. Although *crush* might be more accurate. The sod was attractive enough, as men go, but really. He was the enemy. Kitty lifted Poppy onto her lap and restrained the squirming dog. Uncle Blinker tolerated the Pekingese, but best not to test his patience.

"She found Fredricks?" He dropped the pencil. "Good on her. Where is he?"

"Moscow." She didn't flinch.

"Latest intel coming out of Russia is grim." He sighed. "The Bolsheviks are on the verge of surrendering to Germany." He shuffled some papers. "If they do, we may be next."

Kitty's palms broke out in a cold sweat. Surrender to the Huns? Over her dead body. Poppy licked her face. The pup always had sensed her anxiety. With Poppy's topknot tickling her nose, Kitty couldn't help but laugh.

"This is serious business." His blinking stopped and he stared straight at her. "It is imperative we stop them."

"Yes, Uncle." She held her hand up and Poppy settled back into her lap.

"This is classified and highly sensitive. No one must know." He withdrew a file folder from the stack on his desk. "I'm sending you to rendezvous with Lockhart and Reilly. They're already on the ground." He held out a folder labeled *OA*. "Lieutenant Somersby left for Moscow yesterday."

"Brilliant." Kitty tucked Poppy under her arm and stood up to retrieve the folder. Lieutenant Archie Somersby wasn't going to be very happy when he learned his fiancée had run off after another man, especially when that man was his sworn enemy. She opened the folder and glanced inside. *OA. Operation Ambassadors.*

Uncle Blinker fiddled with a stack of files on his desk. "I will send over a suitable cover for Miss Figg. I know how she loves disguises." He continued rearranging the stack of folders. "Young

Lockhart will fill you in. Steer clear of Reilly if you can. He's a loose cannon." She'd heard of Reilly, of course. Who hadn't? Dashing spy extraordinaire. Leaving a trail of women in his wake.

"Sounds fun." She had butterflies in her stomach. Nothing like the thrill of a new assignment. Hopefully she could find Aunt Fiona before the War Office realized she was missing.

"Be careful." Uncle Blinker frowned. "It's dangerous."

The more dangerous the better. "Of course, Uncle." Kitty smiled sweetly and then leaned over and kissed him on the cheek.

He blushed. "You two come back in one piece."

"Don't worry about us." She stuck the file folder under her arm and held Poppy up like a dolly. "We'll give Fritz a proper bellyache." She kissed the pup's little nose. "Won't we, Poppy-poo?"

2

HAPPY

Ouch. My head hurt. Gingerly, I put a hand to my scalp. I felt the huge goose-egg protruding from my forehead. Those Cheka *pridurki* had hit me with a rifle-butt. I opened my eyes and immediately regretted it. Tears formed as I surveyed the windowless cell, dirty and grimy with who knew what bodily fluids. My stomach turned at the sight of the refuse bucket in the corner. The stench was almost unbearable. Something crawled down my neck and I jumped up. Oh, my word. I'd been lying on a filthy straw mat. The countess was unconscious on a mat next to mine. Five other women were crammed into the small cell. One young woman sat cross-legged on a corner mat. Blood crusted in her hair and across her cheek. Bleary-eyed, she stared out into our bleak future.

"Fredricks," I growled. If I ever got out of here, I was going to hunt him down and throttle him. "*Pridurki*."

"English lady, you speak Russian?" Next to me stood a wiry woman with a wizened face, and baggy clothes. I could tell her tunic hadn't always been so loose. Not to mention her skin. I hated to think what disgusting gruel they served in this rat hole.

"No." I wiped my hands on my skirt.

"Who is this Fredricks you call jerk?" She flashed a broken-toothed smile. "Loverboy?"

"None of your business." I turned away from her. *Loverboy, my eye.*

"Not polite to give back to Rada." She grabbed me by the shoulders. "You nice to Rada and Rada nice to you."

I wriggled free. "And you're Rada?"

She had a strong grip for a small woman. Best not to provoke Rada.

"*Da.*" She flashed her broken smile again. "In English, Rada means Happy. You call me Happy." She smelled like stale onions and weasel.

"Happy." I swallowed back the bile in my throat. "Pleasure to meet you." I cringed as I held out my hand.

"Better," she said, pumping my hand. "I scratch your backside, you scratch me." In the dim light, her broken teeth looked like fangs.

I wasn't going anywhere near her backside. I glanced around at the squalor and despair. I was going to have enough trouble watching my own.

"How old?" Happy poked me with her boney finger.

"How old am I?" I straightened my wig. I must look a complete mess. "Twenty-five going on seventy."

"You think that now." She laughed. "Wait a few months in this *dyre*."

"I won't be here long. I don't belong—"

She cut me off. "None of us belong." She waved a scrawny arm at our cellmates like the usher at a West End curtain call. "You think you special, *Vetka*?"

"No, but..." I sputtered. What if I didn't get out? Surely Fredricks would come looking for me. Did he know I was in prison? Archie certainly wouldn't look for me. He'd given me an ultimatum: marry him now or break it off. It felt like a rock dropped into the pit of my stomach. No one was coming.

"*Vetka*, you and your man Fredricks—" Happy gnawed on her fingernail. I imagined myself doing the same in a month and shuddered. "—have any babies?"

"No." I didn't bother telling her I couldn't have children. That was probably why Andrew had left me for his secretary. He wanted a family, and I couldn't give him one. I was defective. "And Fredricks is not *my man*." *What if Fredricks wants children?* Where did that come from? *Fiona, get a grip.* He was an enemy spy, for heaven's sake... at this very minute negotiating our ally's surrender.

"Twenty-five and no babies. *Vetka*, tsk, tsk." She tutted her tongue. "My babies all grown up and flown. My girl lives in Zurich and my boy in Bristol." Her chest puffed up with pride. "English like you."

"What is *Vetka*?" Probably not a term of endearment.

"Twig." Laughing, she pointed at my torso. "You straight up and down like stick."

I smiled. I'd been called worse.

"Miss Figg, is that you?" The countess sat up on her straw mat. Holding her head, she groaned. "What happened?" She remembered my name, so she couldn't have amnesia.

"The Cheka knocked us out and dragged us here." I helped her to her feet. "This is Rada." I nodded to the Russian.

"Happy," she corrected me.

"This is Countess Brasova."

The countess frowned and put a finger to her lips. "Please," she whispered. "Not in here. I'm just Natasha."

"Countess." Happy bowed her head. "I am honored." She spoke English, no doubt on my account.

The countess got a queer look on her face. "Have I seen you before?" She squinted at Happy. "You look familiar."

"You see me in newspapers." A smile cracked Happy's shriveled face. "My name is Maria Bochkareva, leader of the Women's Battalion of Death." She gave a salute. "At your service."

Women's Battalion of Death. Sounded ominous. Must be a translation issue. Either that or these Russian women were ruthless.

"*Spasibo.* Thank you." The countess grasped the prisoner's dirty hand. "Thank you for defending us." She turned to me. "The Women's Battalion valiantly defended the White Palace against the Bolsheviks."

"We lost." Happy stared down at her worn leather shoes. "Put in jail." Suddenly, she threw her head back. "Not to fear, your grace. Battalion of Death win back Russia and retake throne for tsar."

Happy seemed pretty confident for someone locked up and withering away in a Cheka jail. I wished I could be so sure we'd get out.

* * *

The night was worse than the day. It was impossible to sleep on that infested mat. Women cried and moaned all night. And the smells. Even after forty-eight hours, I wasn't used to the foul stench of the cell. I refused to eat the wormy slop the guards pushed under the bars. Happy finished my portion and Natasha's too. She ate with gusto. Would that be me in another month? My stomach flipped.

All the prisoners deferred to Maria Rada "Happy" Bochkareva. When she spoke, they listened. She talked of escape, of retaking the country, of future glory. She didn't tolerate complaints or crying. She demanded courage. A natural leader, her words inspired us to stay alive. Only at night, when their leader snored, did the other women allow their fears and desperation to overtake them. During the day, Happy recounted battles the Battalion of Death had fought and won, and how the women showed the demoralized men what it meant to stay the course.

Whenever the guards came within earshot, Natasha and I would plead our case. "There's been a misunderstanding. We don't belong here." But Happy was right. No one belonged here. This place was not fit for animals. Every day, Happy reminded us we were not animals, but women. Strong and resourceful women.

After two days in this hellhole, the countess was desperate. "We must get out or I'll go mad." She pulled at her hair. "I'd rather die than stay here."

I knew how she felt. What I wouldn't give for a bath. Or a cup of tea. Or a sip of fresh air. I would never take the simple pleasures of life for granted again. "There must be a way to get out." I closed my eyes to concentrate. Fredrick Fredricks always managed to escape jail. How did he do it? In Paris, he'd feigned paralysis, bided his time, and when the moment presented itself, stole a nun's habit (which I happened to be wearing at the time) and escaped. In New York, he'd slipped out during the chaos of a prisoner transfer. And in Cairo, he'd bribed his way out.

"Can we bribe the guards?" I turned to Natasha. "You must have jewels or money." She was a countess and a royal, after all.

Sorrow filled her dark eyes. "They took everything from me."

"Bribes not work." Happy shook her head. "Guards are fanatics. Hate tsar and money."

"I wasn't born royalty," Natasha said wistfully. "My father was a lawyer."

Happy scoffed. "My father was peasant. I worked as laborer. After husband beat me, I ran away. Had to work in brothel to eat."

Her countenance darkened. "Walked across Siberia to get away." She shook herself like a dog shaking off water. "I not complain. Happy never complain. Just state facts."

We stood in silence for several minutes. No wonder Happy wore her scars as a badge of honor. I couldn't imagine having to sell my body to eat or walk across frozen tundra to safety. Up until now, my life had been grand by comparison.

"Army saved me." Happy broke the silence. "Belief in Russia and tsar saved me. Fighting saved me." She punched the air with a boney fist. "We fight."

"Yes, well, first we need to escape this blasted cell." I pointed out the obvious.

"Twig is right." Happy slapped me on the back. "I have plan." She flashed her crooked smile.

I hoped it didn't involve brothels or walking across Siberia.

She withdrew a spoon from her tunic. "Dig tunnel."

Almost as bad. Her plan involved digging a tunnel with a spoon.

"That will take forever." I sighed. "We'll die in here before we see the light of day."

Happy's face fell. Feeling bad for debunking her plan, I touched her sleeve in consolation. More silence. I paced a step and then had nowhere to go.

"I have a better idea." The countess drew us close. "If we're ill, they'll have to let us out." She doubled over and moaned.

"Ha!" More of Happy's scoffing. She made to slap Natasha's back but thought better of it and balled up her fist. "They not care if we die."

I thought of Fredricks feigning paralysis. If he could devise an escape, so could we. I tried to pace again but could only take two steps before I ran into a filthy mat. There must be a way. I had an idea. "If the guards believe we are contagious and fear for their own lives..." I stomped on something wriggling across the floor. *Disgusting.* "We must convince them we have a deadly disease."

"Tuberculosis." The countess stabbed the air with a well-groomed fingernail.

"Or that new influenza everyone's so afraid of." My friend Clifford had told me about a deadly influenza that started in America and was spreading, killing thousands as it went. For some reason the newspapers were calling it the Spanish Flu.

"Tuberculosis is well known and so are its symptoms." The countess wheezed and faked a cough. "They wouldn't dare let a member of the royal family die in jail." She tore off a strip of her petticoat. "Or the leader of the Women's Battalion."

"What about me?" I picked at the sleeve of my filthy blouse.

"Or a famous British journalist." The countess smiled and continued ripping her petticoat. She was brilliant at subterfuge. No doubt artifice was a prerequisite for royalty. "First, we will remind them of our importance and the consequences of word getting out that we were harmed here."

"Then we get sick." Happy joined in.

"Here." The countess handed us each a piece of white cotton from her petticoat. "Tomorrow, follow my lead."

I tucked the fabric into an empty pocket. The Cheka had confiscated my spy paraphernalia. Had Fredricks found my notebook under the armoire? Or had housekeeping tossed it in a bin?

At least we had a plan. We were no longer just victims. We were actors.

That night, I finally slept.

KITTY'S INTERLUDE
2 MARCH, 11 A.M.

Kitty sat on her suitcase, waiting for the contact in Moscow. Uncle Clifford stood nearby smoking his pipe. Of course, she didn't need a chaperone, but Uncle Blinker had insisted. Uncle Clifford, aka Captain Douglas, was a nice enough fellow, if a bit too hapless for a man in his early forties. She had him wrapped around her little finger, especially when she called him Uncle Clifford. Along with Poppy, they'd taken two trains and an overnight ferry. She and Poppy needed a bath and a hot meal. "A hot meal. Right, Poppy-poo?" She caressed Poppy, and the pup licked her hand. "We're going to find Aunt Fiona and stop the Huns," she whispered into Poppy's topknot. "We'll kick their German arses." An expert in French foot-fighting, Kitty meant it literally. She smiled to herself as she imagined delivering a cart-wheel kick to Vladimir Lenin's face and then another to the back of Kaiser Wilhelm's head.

She glanced around. The bombed-out train station reminded her of the abandoned warehouse where she and her sister used to hide out when they were children, pickpocketing and scrounging for pence and pasties. In those days, Uncle Clifford would have made the perfect target. He'd never suspect a girl was capable of such criminal behavior. If he only knew.

"I say." Uncle Clifford glanced at his watch. "They're late. You don't suppose something has happened."

In the chaos that was Russia these days, anything could happen. They could have been arrested, or deported, or executed. It was a wonder the Russians allowed the British to keep their embassy open. Kitty fiddled with Poppy's bow. From what she'd read in the top-secret file, it was only a matter of days until the Bolsheviks surrendered to the Germans and gave up the Baltic governorates. That was a massive loss of territory. And the loss of one of Britain's most important allies on the Eastern Front. "Don't worry, Uncle Clifford." She smiled sweetly. "I'm sure they'll be along soon." And as soon as they were, she could ditch Uncle Clifford and find Aunt Fiona. No sense in exposing Fiona's folly to the world. Especially to Clifford, who had a well-earned reputation as a tattletale.

"Why don't we take a taxi to the hotel?" Puffing on his pipe, Uncle Clifford scratched Poppy under the chin. "I want to surprise Fiona." As far as he knew, they were meeting Aunt Fiona at the Metropol. Yeah. He was the one in for a surprise.

"I can't wait to see Aunt Fiona, too." Kitty held Poppy out to him. Uncle Clifford couldn't resist the pup. "But Uncle Blinker said to wait for Lockhart, so maybe we should wait a bit longer."

Clifford took the dog into his arms and cooed at the squirming bundle of fur. Where was young Lockhart? Kitty tapped her foot. She wasn't used to waiting.

"Captain Douglas?" A tall man with a flat face, wide nose, and one sleepy eye held out his hand.

Kitty stood up and brushed the wrinkles out of her wool coat. "Hello, Mr. Lockhart." From the top-secret file, she'd learned Sir Robert Hamilton Bruce Lockhart (R. H. B. L.) was British Consul

General in Moscow and the ringleader for Operation Ambassadors. Young Lockhart didn't look much older than her. With his slicked-back hair and bow-tie, he could have been a college laddie hanging around the pub waiting for a game of snooker.

"You must be Blinker's niece." His smile was warm and disarming. Not a bad-looking chap. No doubt a good spy for it. Not as good as her, but still.

She took a deep breath and began the performance. Giggling, she held out a gloved hand. "Kitty Lane. Nice to meet you." She batted her lashes. No one ever suspected a pretty girl of deceit and espionage, especially when she wore a frilly pinafore and talked baby-talk to an adorable Pekingese dressed in a matching outfit. "Meet Poppy." She reached over and held up the dog's paw. "Poppy-poo, say hello to Mr. Lockhart."

3

COLD SHOWER

The next morning, when the guards came to give us our gruel, Natasha leaned against the bars, coughing. She sounded downright consumptive. When one of the guards came over to see what was wrong, the countess coughed into the white cotton fabric she'd ripped from her petticoat and then produced the blood-stained cloth. So that was what she had planned for the bits of petticoat. Clever. Her performance was impressive. She'd almost convinced *me* she had tuberculosis.

When she collapsed in a heap, the guard called out to his mate. Holding the rest of the women back with bayonets, one of the guards carried the countess out of the cell. Her head bobbing as he went, she opened one eye just before they disappeared down the hall. Her plan had worked. At least she was out of the cell. But where were they taking her?

"Where did she get the blood?" I asked Happy.

"Where do you think?" Happy's hand gestures caught the attention of one of the guards. He barked something in Russian. Making lewd gestures, Happy barked right back.

"A bit spunky for a consumptive," I whispered.

"What is spunky consumptive?" Happy asked.

"Energetic." I gave a little cough. "Sick."

"Watch me, Twig." She winked at me. "You learn something." She coughed, slapped her knee, and coughed some more. Then she fell to the floor in convulsions. The guard laughed and pumped the air with his bayonet. Clearly amused, he moved closer for a better view. Happy flopped around like a fish out of water. I knelt next to her and screamed for help. Eventually, some of the guards took pity, either that or they wanted to stop her ruckus. One grabbed her arms and another her feet and together they dragged her away. I heard Happy cackling from the hallway. She'd taken the first step back to the Battalion of Death.

It seemed unlikely that the guards would fall for the sickness ruse a third time. So, I bided my time until supper. When the guards returned with the slop that passed for stew, I started hacking. As one of the guards slid a bowl under the bars, I fell to my knees in a fit of coughing that shook my entire body. My acting classes back at North London Collegiate School for Girls came in handy. Now for the hard part. I took a deep breath and bit down on my lip. Face to face with the guard, I spat into the makeshift handkerchief and made sure he saw the blood. He stared at me, and I coughed in his face. He recoiled and shouted something in Russian. A few minutes later, two guards were carrying me out of the cell. A chorus of coughing followed me down the hall. The guards loaded me into a lorry. I didn't know where they were taking me, but it couldn't be any worse than that filthy jail cell.

After a short ride in the lorry, I was jostled into a well-guarded, squat building. The foul stench of the jail was replaced by the strong smells of bleach and ether. The guards carried me on a stretcher through a corridor and into a small barren room and then rolled me off onto the cold, damp floor. Other than a drain in the center of the floor and a coiled hose, the room was windowless and completely empty. The guards left and bolted the door from the outside. I lay there in the dark for a few seconds, waiting for my eyes to adjust. Impossible. The blackness was all encompassing. Shivering, I sat up and hugged my knees to my chest. Was this a gas chamber? Was I about to be executed?

After what seemed like hours, the lock clicked, and the door swung open. Like a mole poking its head out of a hole at high noon, I was blinded by the bright light streaming in from the hallway. I shielded my eyes and tried to focus on three figures who'd just entered the tiny room. One of them said something in Russian. A woman. My eyes adjusted enough to make out their white uniforms and caps. Three nurses. Were these nurses my executioners?

The largest of the three grabbed me and started stripping off my blouse.

"What do you think you're doing?" I struggled to free myself from her tight grip on my arm. "You're hurting me."

She ignored me and continued ripping at my clothes. A second nurse pulled my skirt off.

Trembling, I lay on the floor in my smalls. "No!" I shouted as the largest nurse tore off my underwear. I curled up into a naked ball. "Ahhhh," I screamed. The third nurse had turned on the hose and was spraying me with ice-cold water. The other two scrubbed me with a bar of lye soap. The biting smell was familiar to me from the lye my grandmother used on the farm to clean the floors. My skin turned bright red and stung like the dickens. By the time the nurses finished hosing me off, I was shaking violently. Even Happy's performance in the jail didn't match my convulsions. One of the nurses left the room and reappeared seconds later with a small sheet. She barked something in Russian and threw it at me. The cloth was coarse and thin, but I dried myself as best as I could. The large nurse grabbed me under the arms and lifted me to my feet while her comrade tugged a long burlap tunic over my head. My bath may not have been all that I'd hoped for, but at least I was clean and bug-free.

The nurses lifted me into a chair on wheels and rolled me down a long hallway and into an infirmary. The long narrow room was divided by flimsy curtains. On either side, rows of cots lined the yellowing walls. In the center, a long metal table held stacks of bedpans, water pitchers, and various medical instruments. A uniformed, armed guard leaned on a cabinet, using the tip of his bayonet to clean his fingernails.

A team of nurses tied me to a cot. I thrashed and protested to no avail. After they'd secured me to the metal frame, they vanished. What little freedom of movement I had in the jail, I'd traded for a clean bed. At least I hoped it was clean. I didn't feel any creepy-crawlies and the mattress wasn't on the floor. So, that was an improvement.

Were Natasha and Happy here, too? I tried to survey the room, but the restraints and the curtains prevented me from seeing anything except the vacant cot directly across from mine.

"Natasha," I called out. "Happy?" The only response came from the other side of the closest curtain. A woman speaking Russian. "I don't speak Russian." I repeated the phrase in French and then in garbled German.

"Keep your voice down," the woman drawled. "Or the guard will be on you like an Alabama deer tick." The American's thick southern accent made it difficult to understand her.

"I'm Fiona, who are you?" I tried to sit up, but it was no use. I was attached to the bed like—what had she said—an Alabama deer tick.

"Peggy from Missouri." The way she said it sounded like miss-sir-a. "Or as I call it, misery. What'd they get you for?"

"Wrong place at the wrong time," I stage-whispered.

"Tell me about it." Peggy sighed. "I'm a journalist, how about you?"

"File clerk." I couldn't tell her I was a spy. "From London." I twisted my head toward the curtain. I could make out Peggy's silhouette in the next cot. Was she tied down, too?

"I figured you were British from your accent." Her silhouette sat up. No, not tied down. How did she manage to get free? "Do you have any news about what's going on with the Bolsheviks?"

"Only that they might surrender to the Germans." I hoped I wasn't betraying some British military secret.

The silhouette stood up and then disappeared. The curtain fluttered. A face popped up next to mine. Peggy had crawled around the curtain and was kneeling next to my cot—her pencil brows arched, a smile playing on her thin lips, and her snub nose just inches from my own. "Have they moved their headquarters yet?" she whispered. Her hair was a nest of brown curls and she smelled of lilacs and lye.

I twisted my neck to get a better look at her. "I don't know." Natasha hadn't mentioned the government moving. Everything seemed to be constantly moving on the political scene in Russia. It was deuced confusing, with so many factions jockeying for power and everything in flux.

"Afraid of the tsarists in Petrograd." When she smiled, her dark eyes sparkled like a wood nymph from a fairytale. "Lenin is moving government headquarters here, to Moscow." Peggy set to work untying me from the cot. *Thank goodness.* "Word on the street is..." She slid under my cot and reached up to untie my other side. "The tsar's brother escaped and is leading the resistance."

The tsar's brother. "Michael?" Did Natasha know her husband had escaped? I had to find her and tell her.

"Yes." She popped up on the side of my cot again. "There, better?"

I sat up and rubbed my wrists. "Much."

"I have to hide these." She held up a loose tie and then unhooked it and hid it under the blanket at the foot of my cot. "Those linebackers won't be back."

"Linebackers?"

"That big one could have played for the Jayhawks." She finished hiding the ties and then settled cross-legged on the floor next to my cot, brushing her hands together a few times.

I gave her a blank look.

"My hometown football team." She shrugged. "Never mind." Peeking up over the cot, she pulled a small, wrapped bar from the sleeve of her tunic. "Want one?" She held it out on her palm. A sweetie in a blue wrapper illustrated with four bears on a tree trunk. "I'm friendly with one of the guards." She smiled. "He's sweet on me."

I took it, unwrapped it, and took a bite. "Hmmm."

"Clumsy Bear are the best. These are last year's model. The Soviets took over the factory and now they're called Red October."

"A rose by any other name." Praline filling between two waffle sheets covered in dark chocolate. Scrummy. I devoured the rest. Only then did I realize just how hungry I was. I hadn't eaten in days.

"I hope you like beets," she said. "That's all we get to eat in here."

"How long have you been here?"

A rustling near the door made her freeze. Her eyes went wide, and she put a finger to her lips.

We both sat at attention, listening. Nothing.

She relaxed back against the wall. "Four days."

"They transferred me from jail." My stomach growled.

"I can tell." She pointed to the red bumps on my forearm. "I was reporting on some action in the square and got grazed by a bullet." She touched a bandage on her leg. "No big deal really. But the Cheka gathered me up and threw me in here."

"Where is here?" I couldn't see out of the lorry and had no idea where they'd taken me.

"Soldatenkov Military Hospital, special wing for women prisoners." She picked at her bandage. "I don't know what happens next."

"Yesterday, did they bring in an attractive woman in her late twenties?" I leaned back on my elbows. "Perhaps you would have recognized her as Countess Brasova?"

"Countess Brasova." She furrowed her brow. "Natalia Romanov? Here? Why?"

"We were incarcerated together, along with another Russian woman called Rada. But they were removed from our cell yesterday after feigning illness."

"Countess Brasova, here?" She grimaced. "That's not good."

"Why not?" I pulled the blanket up around my shoulders.

"She might as well have a target on her back." Peggy shook her head. "The Cheka will come looking for her."

"We need to find her and warn her." I pulled my knees up to my chest. "And tell her about her husband."

"Hopefully just rumors." She sighed. "Michael is not nearly as bad as his tyrant brother. Still, the monarchy is a thing of the past. Why should a handful of pretenders control the wealth of an entire nation? Shouldn't everyone get a piece of the pie?"

My stomach growled. Did she have to say pie? "What's so bad about the tsar?"

"He treated *his* people terribly. Bled them dry with taxes until they had nothing." She shook her head. "Disgusting, really. The

Bolsheviks are just what Russia needs to get rid of the taste of tyranny."

Peggy was the first person I'd heard praising the Bolsheviks.

Except for Fredricks. He'd closed his letter with a postscript endorsing Lenin's slogan, "Peace, bread, and land." Right before his second postscript referring to my would-be engagement to Archie:

If you change your mind, join me at Metropol Hotel, Suite 315.
I offer you only the world.

Right. Thanks to Fredricks, my world had been reduced to a stinking jail and being hog-tied to a cot.

KITTY'S INTERLUDE
3 MARCH, NOON

The ambassador's forest-green Vauxhall motorcar was very fancy with its three rows of seats and shiny brass. But the British consulate was nothing more than a dingy flat at the back of a shabby building. Kitty didn't know why she'd expected more. The War Office in the Old Admiralty building was downright posh by comparison. The consulate was barely furnished. Two empty desks, a bookcase, and a large table sat in the center of the room like someone had just dropped them off and no one had bothered to properly arrange them. The small kitchenette had a kettle and two cups and nothing more. There was a sparsely furnished bedroom and a small bathroom. Was the consulate a front for something else?

Robert introduced her to his overdressed partner Sidney Reilly, who, after some cajoling, agreed to talk openly in her presence. Sidney Reilly, known to insiders as "The Ace" because he was the best spy, despite his reputation as a con man and womanizer. She could see how his slicked-back hair and easy smile had appeal. And his notch-lapeled dinner jacket and gold cuff-links were his tickets to high society. To reassure him, Kitty sat on a small sofa in the corner petting Poppy, pretending not to listen as the men formulated their plan. The more she giggled and played with her puppy, the more they ignored her, which was exactly what she wanted. To them, she was a silly girl with an even sillier dog. Little did they know, she and her dog were highly trained operatives. With the proper command, Poppy could slice a man's throat with the sharp diamond on her collar—providing the man held still.

In the center of the room, five men stood around the table. Besides British agents Robert Lockhart and Sidney Reilly, there was a boastful Russian revolutionary named Boris Savinkov who fancied himself a novelist and claimed to be an advisor to former British Home Secretary Winston Churchill. He wore a high-collared military uniform and never removed his cap. He had the hawklike eyes of an assassin and the slumped shoulders of a disillusioned soldier—a disillusioned assassin, the most dangerous kind. The fifth, of course, was Uncle Clifford, who stood back smoking his pipe, interjecting a hunting story whenever he got the chance, which wasn't often. These men didn't waste time.

"Only by cutting off its head can we stop the beast." Sidney Reilly pounded the table with his fist. Reilly assured them that the Ambassador Plot, as he'd called it, had the green light from the War Office and that he'd secured access to the highest levels of the Bolshevik government. "We'll kidnap Lenin and Trotsky and execute them."

"The Russian people don't want the Bolsheviks." Boris put both hands on the table and leaned forward. "And not because the bastards shoot them and steal their grain. But for the simple reason that no one elected them."

"Agreed. We've got to take them out and keep Russia fighting on our side." Despite his age, Robert Lockhart had a commanding presence. He spoke with the authority of a British lord.

Admirable. A force to be reckoned with. Much like herself. After the entire plan was on the table, under the pretext of taking Poppy out "for a wee," Kitty left the consulate and went in search of Aunt Fiona. She was glad for the bitter cold after the stifling masculinity of the consulate.

Unfortunately, the only picture she had of Aunt Fiona was a fake identification card made by the War Office. In it, Fiona was dressed as Rear Admiral Arbuthnot. Unless Fredrick was into something kinky, Aunt Fiona wouldn't be wearing trousers and a mustache on a romantic holiday.

The MHM, Metropol Hotel Moscow, was just across the river. She turned up the collar of her coat and tugged on Poppy's leash. Heading into the wind, her ears burned. Aunt Fiona would have reminded her to wear a hat. She picked up her pace. By the time she arrived at the hotel, her fingers were like icicles.

The grand entrance with its high glass dome, crystal chandeliers, and marble fountain gave hints of its former glory—before the Bolsheviks and tsarists had it out in the town square. Once inside, she made a beeline to the fireplace. She held out her hands to the flames. Ahh. Her muscles relaxed. Poppy shook the cold off her fur. After a few minutes of enjoying the warmth, they trotted across the grand lobby to the reception desk. Speaking fluent Russian, Kitty asked the clerk at the desk if a Miss Fiona Figg or a Mr. Fredrick Fredricks were guests. He blinked at her.

She described Aunt Fiona. Tall, thin, prominent chin, perfect hair. She didn't mention it looked perfect because it was a wig; Fiona kept her head shorn to wear her disguises. The clerk glanced around nervously and then shook his head.

"And the man?" She described Fredricks. Over six feet, muscular, looks like he could wrestle a Siberian tiger. A master of disguises, Fredricks could have any color hair and any style of dress. But he couldn't hide his bulky form.

The clerk shook his head again.

She asked if she might look around, and he nodded and then disappeared into the back office. Obviously, the clerk wasn't one to stand up to interrogation. He'd probably dealt with armed revolutionaries, Cossacks, Bolsheviks, and tsarists. She knew better than to underestimate him. And yet she sensed he was lying. But why?

Kitty asked the maids and kitchen staff if they'd seen Fiona. No one had seen a tall nosey English lady with a penchant for trouble. Neither would they admit to hosting the infamous German spy. She sneaked up the back stairs to check out suite 315. The room Fredrick mentioned in his letter. To her surprise, the occupant was a Latvian baker visiting his daughter in Moscow. The man had a bulbous nose and a hairy mole on his forehead. He refused to let her into the suite, insisting he'd never seen the man Kitty described.

No sign of Fredricks. Damn him. The sod had taken Aunt Fiona and run off. They could be halfway around the world by now. But they weren't. Her gut told her they were here. Russia was on the brink of a peace treaty with Germany. Not one to be side-lined, Fredricks would be at the center of the action. He was here somewhere. And so was Aunt Fiona. But where?

With Poppy in tow, she marched back down the stairs, back outside, and back across the river. "Wherever you are, Aunt Fiona, I hope you're enjoying yourself."

4

REUNION

I never saw those "linebacker" nurses again. Peggy was right—even if she was also a Bolshevik sympathizer. I had to learn to keep my big mouth shut. Russia was like a prism with so many sides you didn't know what color you'd end up with or how the light would refract. I only hoped I hadn't betrayed Countess Brasova. She and Happy were my only friends in this godforsaken country. I'd been in the infirmary for days and hadn't seen hide nor hair of them. And yet where else could they be? According to Peggy, all sick or injured women prisoners were transferred here to Soldatenkov Military Hospital.

Short-staffed, like hospitals all over the war-torn world, nurses did rounds only once a day and doctors were scarce. A quiet girl served us two meals a day, mostly thin potato or beet soup. But at least none of it squirmed in the bowl. After starving in jail, even the watery soups were welcome. Thankfully, no one had offered to tie me to my cot again. In fact, except for the night nurse poking or prodding every evening, we were left to our own devices. As long as we were quiet, the armed guard was too busy with his magazines to pay us much mind. The minute we tried to

walk across the room or peek out a window, he was on us like an
Alabama tick, as Peggy would say.

That evening for dinner, we got a crust of bread with our
soup. It was stale and heavy, but it was my first solid food in days.

Slurping her soup, next to my cot, Peggy sat on the floor so the
guard couldn't see her. "You need it more than I do." She handed
me her bread. I refused it. She insisted until I gave up and tucked
into it with gusto. Despite her queer political leanings, Peggy was
a good sort.

A commotion at the door made me prick up my ears. I got out
of bed and tiptoed to the edge of the curtain and peeked around.

A nurse was conferring with the guard. They were both bent
over a clipboard. When the nurse glanced in my direction, I
disappeared back behind the curtain and held my breath. I'd
heard stories of misbehaving women being thrown back in jail or
worse.

The guard positioned himself in the center of the room and
read off the clipboard, calling out names. "Schmidt, Bauer,
Müller." As he did, women stepped out from behind their
curtains and into the aisle.

"What's happening?" I whispered.

"I don't know." Peggy clutched the collar of her tunic. "Either
they're being transferred to another facility or..." Her voice trailed
off. She didn't need to say it. Or they were being rounded up for
execution.

"Fischer, Becker, Wagner..." The guard continued reading
names. And women, some of them hobbling or bandaged, lined
up in the center of the room. The point of his bayonet leading the
way, he marched the women out of the room.

Listening to the sounds of footfalls in the hallway, Peggy and I
finished the rest of our soup in silence, except for an occasional
slurp. We waited for the quiet girl to come back to retrieve the

dishes. She never came. No one did. Not even the night nurse. Eventually, my curiosity got the better of me, and I peeked around the curtain again. The guard was gone. And the noise from the hallway had stopped.

"Peggy, there's no guard." I tentatively took a step out from behind the curtain. The infirmary was quiet except for a few soft moans or whispers from behind one of the curtains. A ray of moonlight cut across the floor as if marking our escape route. I ventured a few more steps. "They're all gone," I stage-whispered.

Peggy joined me in the moonlight. "Let's skedaddle before the guard gets back." She bolted toward the door.

I followed her. Barefoot and wearing only burlap tunics, even if we could escape the hospital, we wouldn't last long outside in the frigid night air. We needed to find clothes and shoes. And I planned to find the countess and Happy. I couldn't abandon them. Not after they'd helped me escape that awful jail cell.

The hallway was dimly lit, but empty of guards or staff. Something was going on, but what? Had the Bolshevik regime toppled? Russian governments were falling like dominos. Had the Russians surrendered Moscow to the Germans? Surely not. Why move the capital from Petrograd to Moscow just to hand it over to the enemy? That was the problem. If Russia signed a peace treaty with Germany, then they would be allies, not enemies. Would that make Russia our enemy, too?

My mind racing, I followed Peggy. The stone floor was cold against my bare feet. I hugged my tunic close to my naked torso. For all the good it did. I was still freezing and exposed. If I had to face armed men, I'd rather do it with a thick pair of woolen trousers. Like one of the disguises that were hanging in my closet back at the Metropol Hotel. Crikey. If the management hadn't thrown them out by now.

At the end of the hall, I caught up to Peggy in a stairwell. "I've got to find my friends."

"Suit yourself." Her tunic flying, she took the stairs two at a time. "Try this floor." She pointed at a door on her way past it. "Tubercular women's ward."

"Good luck," I called after her.

She disappeared down the stairs.

Slowly, I opened the door just a crack and peeked through. The coast was clear, so I dashed into the hallway. There were four doors, which one was the tuberculosis ward? Luckily, on the train ride from London to Moscow, I'd memorized the Cyrillic alphabet and the words in my *Hill's Russian-English vest-pocket dictionary*. The second door was marked *туберкулез*. Close enough. Carefully, I opened it and stepped inside. No guards here either. How odd.

I was met with a chorus of coughing. Like the war, tuberculosis didn't discriminate. It took the rich and the poor. Although, when infected, wealthy Londoners took to posh spas in the mountains while the poor died in the streets. I did my best to hold my breath. My grandmother used to say I was as healthy as a horse. I hoped she was right.

"Natasha." I dashed from one cot to the next. "Happy. Are you here?"

The women patients stared at me, some of them asking for help, others just groaning, and one screaming like she'd seen a ghost.

"Natasha?" I glided along the floor. "Happy?"

"Twig?" A voice came from behind a middle curtain. "Where you at?" I followed the sound. "Come play." Happy and three other women were sitting on the floor, using a cot as a table to play cards.

"Am I ever glad to see you." I put my hand on her shoulder.

"We play for bread." She flashed her crooked smile. "You in?" After just a few days in the infirmary, her cheeks had filled out and she'd put on weight. She looked good, and in her element.

"I'm out." I glanced around at the other women and then leaned over and whispered in her ear, "The guards are gone, we need to get out of here, now. Where's Natasha?"

"Countess," Happy yelled. "Twig's here."

My cheeks warmed. Wasn't she worried about the guards or waking the other patients?

"These ladies from Battalion of Death." Happy stood up and spoke in Russian. The card players nodded and smiled. "Wounded protecting palace." She puffed out her chest. "Brave like mama bear." She slapped me on the shoulder. "We get countess."

I put my finger to my lips.

"English lady," she scoffed. "Not brave."

There is a fine line between bravery and recklessness. I nodded. "Let's find Natasha and get out of here while we can." This was no time to argue.

Looking me in the eyes, a smile playing on her lips, she shouted again, "Countess." The way she carried on, we would be lucky if we weren't hauled in front of a firing squad.

Her eyes full of sleep, Natasha poked her head around the curtain. When she saw me, her face lit up. "Miss Fiona Figg. I wondered what became of you." She gave me a hug. "I thought your friend the duke would have sprung you by now." Tilting her head, she held me at arm's length. "What have you heard from him?"

The duke, aka Fredrick Fredricks, was why I was in this mess in the first place. And, no, he hadn't sprung me. And no, I hadn't heard from him. I shook my head. I had no idea where he was or what he was doing. But I was beginning to suspect the blackguard had lured me to Moscow on false pretenses. His grand plan was to leave me to rot in a Soviet jail.

"Ah, yes." The countess squinted at me. "Your friend is working with the Bolsheviks on the treaty." Her mood was as changeable as the March sky. Not that I'd seen the sky, lately. "They're holding the royal family hostage in Tobolsk. Threatening to kill them if we don't bow down." She picked at her fingernail. "We're their insurance policy against tsarist insurrection." She glanced up into my eyes. "And you're here to spy for them." I didn't blame the countess for being paranoid. Her husband and in-laws were being rounded up and carted off to Siberia.

"Me, a spy?" I swallowed hard. Alright. I was a spy. Past tense. I needn't bother going back to the War Office. I was most certainly sacked. If I didn't die in Russia first. "Come on." I tugged at Natasha's tunic. "We've got to get out of here."

The countess stood staring over my shoulder, her mouth working but no sound coming out. A man's voice boomed right behind my head. My hands flew to my ears. I spun around and was face to face with an angry guard. He was shouting in Russian and waving his bayonet.

Happy countered with fist shaking and yelling of her own. Within seconds, the guard was joined by three more. The countess gave me the evil eye, like it was my fault. By my accounts, it was her fault. I shouldn't have gone looking for her. I should have left with Peggy, who was probably in some pub enjoying a hot toddy by now.

One of the guards spoke to Natasha. The only thing I could make out was "Countess Brasova." She held her head high as he "escorted" her out of the room. The other three guards carted the rest of us off to a cold, dark, dank, and very small room in the basement. A bit crowded for solitary. Seemed more like an empty storage room. It smelled of rotting vegetables, dirt, and death. The only place to sit was on an overturned five-gallon bucket and we had to take turns.

Happy and her crew weren't happy. The guards had confiscated their cards and, down here, we'd be lucky to get any food, let alone bread to wager. But instead of complaining, which was always my go-to in times of trouble, they stumbled around in the dark, feeling their way, looking for possible escape routes. Even after they confirmed that we were trapped in a stone box, they still didn't grumble. Happy "not complain." Unhappy, I did.

"When guard comes back, we jump on him." Happy took charge.

I didn't relish the thought of a bayonet to the gut, but she was right. We had to take our chances. We couldn't stay in here. "What's going on tonight? Where did the guards go? Where did they take the countess?"

"You don't know?" Happy sounded incredulous.

I shook my head.

"This morning, Bolsheviks sign over Russia to Germany." Happy's torso deflated like a balloon. "My country not the same."

"The peace treaty." Fredricks had succeeded. He'd always said he was working for peace. And, as I always suspected, it was at Britain's expense.

"Not peace." Happy shook her fist. "Surrender."

"What's the date today?" I counted in my head. Locked up for who knows how long, I'd completely lost track of time.

"Sunday, 3 March." Happy glared at me. "History will remember day Bolsheviks betrayed Russia and our allies."

Sunday, 3 March. The date on Fredricks's matchbox. How did he know? And those names the guard read off the clipboard. I realized what they had in common. They were all German names. Of course. Once they signed the peace treaty, the Russians

freed all the German prisoners of war. That explained the footfalls in the hallway for an hour. If there was that much chaos in
here, imagine how much there must be out on the streets.

With the peace treaty concluded, was Fredricks back at the
Metropol? Had he found my notebook? Would he come looking
for me?

While the men were out gathering ammunition and weapons for
Operation Ambassadors, Kitty returned to the Metropol Hotel.
Since the Bolsheviks had signed the so-called peace treaty with
Germany three days ago, Fiona could be in even more trouble.
Moscow was in chaos and the Cheka was more violent and brutal
than ever.

Kitty was determined to find someone who would tell her the
truth. This time, she took Aunt Fiona's wig along. If the staff
wouldn't tell her Fiona's whereabouts, Poppy would. "Right,
Poppy-poo?" She held the wig in front of the pup's nose. "You'll
track Aunt Fiona." With her adorable little face, she might not
look it, but Poppy was a highly skilled operative. Despite her flat
nose, Poppy could track a scent. She was just a bit snortier than
your average blood hound.

The hotel clerk scowled when Kitty approached the desk. He
pretended to be busy with some paperwork, but she knew better.
Forget about that lying clerk. Kitty kept going and crossed the
lobby to the lift. She'd find a helpful maid or a loose-lipped
porter. She exited the lift on the third floor and returned to suite

315. If Fredricks had made a point of including the suite number, he'd done it for a reason.

Preparing her story for the Latvian baker, she knocked on the door. She would tell him that her aunt had lost a valuable bracelet when she'd stayed in this same suite a few days ago. She just wanted to come in and look for it. Wouldn't take more than a few minutes. The baker didn't answer the door. No one did. She knocked again. Even better. No need for stories. She could simply help herself without anyone looking over her shoulder. Aunt Fiona wasn't the only one with a lockpick set. Russian locks were no match for Kitty. She manipulated the tension wrench and the rake, and voila, the door opened.

The suite was empty. The baker had vacated. All the better. She could take her time. Poppy trotted in after her and she closed the door. Now, where to start? She pulled Aunt Fiona's wig out of her haversack and gave Poppy another sniff. She patted the pup, who gazed up at her with undying devotion. "Good girl." Poppy wasn't just her espionage partner, but the love of her life. She smiled down at her little friend. "Now get to work." She gave the pup a hand command. "Find her."

Nose down, tail up, Poppy circumnavigated the suite. Kitty trailed after the pup, looking behind the dresser and under the bed as she went. Maybe the cleaning staff had missed something. Poppy ran past the closet without stopping. Kitty opened it anyway. Fredricks had been there. His ridiculous hunting outfit hung in the closet, along with those tall black boots he always wore. Why were his clothes still here? Had he come back after the Latvian baker? Or was the Latvian baker covering for Fredricks? Poppy stopped near the door in front of an armoire and started barking. Kitty knelt on the floor and then peeked underneath. A notebook. She reached under and dragged it out.

Aunt Fiona's notebook. Proof she'd been in this very suite.

Kitty read the last page aloud. "Brest-Litovsk at the Bug River ala Countess Brasova." Brest-Litovsk. Where Trotsky and the gang were conspiring with the Germans to sign the peace treaty. Countess Brasova was the tsar's sister-in-law, Natalia Romanov. Why had Fiona written her name in the notebook? Far from being involved with the peace treaty, Natalia Romanov had a vested interest in restoring the monarchy. Obviously, Aunt Fiona had some reason to pursue Countess Brasova.

Kitty turned the notebook over in her hands. Scratched across the front was one word written in thick crooked letters, "CHE-KA." The Russian secret police. The handwriting looked like that of a child first learning to write her alphabet. She opened the notebook and flipped through the pages. Notes on their various assignments. Inside, the handwriting was neat and tight, very much like Aunt Fiona herself. Either someone else had scrawled "CHEKA" across the front of the notebook, or Aunt Fiona dashed it off in a fantastic hurry. But why?

Kitty squeezed her eyes shut. "No. No. No." She knew why, and it wasn't pretty. Her stomach sank. If the Cheka had Aunt Fiona, then who knew *where* she was... or *if* she was. Kitty slapped the notebook against her palm.

Olga Alexandrov. She would know. Olga was a Russian girl who'd been at Kitty's espionage school in France. Last Kitty had heard she was working for French military intelligence, the *Deuxième Bureau*, and had infiltrated the Cheka.

"Come on, Poppy." She pulled on the pup's leash.

Olga was Kitty's only chance to find Aunt Fiona. Hopefully, before it was too late.

5

THE PLAN

I listened to Happy's plan. We would take turns watching by the door, night or day. And if someone heard a guard approach, they would signal the others. Then we would split into two groups of three on either side of the door—me and the smallest of Happy's crew behind the door, and Happy and her other two soldiers on the other side. The plan was to bring our clenched fists down on the guard's head as soon as he stepped through the door. It sounded like madness. Six half-naked women flailing away in the dark. But I didn't have a better plan.

We'd been locked up in the basement storage room for who-knew-how-long with only a plate of stale bread thrown to us now and then like we were dogs. We had turned over the bucket and designated one corner for the call of nature. Our growling stomachs distracted from the darkness, the smells, and everything else about the nasty place. Out of the frying pan into the fire. Why did I have to go looking for the countess? I should have minded my own business and stuck with Peggy.

It was my turn to sit by the door with my ears pricked. The other women leaned against the side wall, huddled together for warmth, and attempted sleep. None of us knew any more whether it was night or day. And though we were all exhausted, it wasn't easy to sleep—not knowing when, or if, you'd get your next meal or be hauled in front of a firing squad. I was beginning to think the guards had forgotten about us. Either that, or they planned to let us rot down here.

Click. Click. Click. A tapping sound was getting closer. Footfalls. A woman's heels. A guard or a nurse? I was tempted to give up on Happy's plan and pound on the door. What if she passed us by without opening the door? What if she didn't know we were in here? Should I tell the others? Or pound on the door and scream? I listened again to confirm I wasn't hearing things.

I wasn't. The footfalls were getting closer.

Click. Click. Click. Yes, they were almost to the door.

"Happy," I whispered. "Someone's coming."

The women got to their feet. We took up our positions. I raised my fists over my head, ready to bring them down as soon as the door opened. My heart was racing. The adrenaline coursing through my veins compensated for my weakness from lack of food.

Behind me, I could feel one of the women's breath on my neck. She had her arms raised above my head. Huddled together, we prepared our attack.

"Moment door opens," Happy whispered. "Crack."

The footfalls stopped on the other side of the door. Another tinnier clicking continued. Not as loud but at a faster interval. Nails on stone. A tiny Battalion of Death? I held my breath and prepared to bring my fists down on the first head through that door.

Wait. What? The clicking was replaced by barking. A dog. Not a big dog but the yapping of a small dog. Lowering my arms, I put my ear to the door. Scratching noises rose from the bottom of the door and from higher up the tinkling of someone jimmying the lock.

Why would the guard need to pick the lock? The yipping didn't sound like the bark of a guard dog. I knew that bark.

"Poppy?" I stepped in front of the door.

More yapping and scratching at the door.

"Aunt Fiona, is that you?" Kitty's familiar voice was a balm to my soul.

"Kitty and Poppy!" I laughed. "At ease, soldiers. I know that dog."

* * *

The door swung open. Wearing black from head to toe, Kitty stood feet apart, hands raised, ready to attack. When she saw me, she relaxed her stance.

"Aunt Fiona!" She clapped her hands together.

I was never so glad to see a girl and her dog in my life. Poppy jumped up my leg until I bent down and scooped her up. "Poppy, am I glad to see you."

"She led me right to you." Kitty pulled one of my wigs out of a back pocket and shook it at me.

I snatched it out of her hand. "Where did you get that?"

"From your flat." She smiled.

"In London?" What in heaven's name was she doing in my flat?

"Do you have any other?" She raised her eyebrows.

"I'm Happy." She held out her hand. "What is that?" Happy pointed at the dog. "Otter?"

"I'm happy too." Kitty glanced over her shoulder. "I'd love to chit-chat, but right now—"

"Let's get out of here." I stepped out into the hallway. After the dark storage room, the lights in the hall scalded my eyeballs. I shielded my eyes with my hand.

"This way." Kitty led us down the hall toward a steel door.

Behind the door was a stairwell. Quietly, we ascended from the basement. When we reached the door to the ground floor, Kitty held up her hand. We all stood still as statues. I pricked up my ears. There were voices coming from the other side of the door. We waited. My pulse quickened. I glanced over at Happy. Chomping at the bit, she balled up her fists. As soon as the voices receded, Kitty motioned toward the door. Carefully, I gripped the doorknob and slowly turned it. A click made me stop. Grimacing, I sucked in air and then continued. I opened the door a crack and peeked out. At the far end of the hall, armed guards stood outside the doors to the prisoners' wards. Carrying a stack of clean towels, a nurse scurried up the hall in our direction. Kitty slid past me and through the door. Carrying Poppy, I slipped out behind her. Single file, the other women followed.

Kitty stopped and whispered, "Move out in front of me and follow my lead."

Did she want us to lead or follow? I did as she bade and stepped in front of her. She pulled a gun from an inside jacket pocket and pushed it into my back. I recognized that gun. The pearl-handled gun Mata Hari had given me in Paris. How did Kitty get my gun?

"What is this?" Happy protested.

"I trust her." I beckoned to my fellow prisoners. "Do as she says if you want to get out of here alive." I didn't tell her that Kitty was a highly trained British operative. Or that she'd once tied me to a toilet.

Happy scowled. Obviously, she was used to giving orders and not taking them.

"*Podvin' eto!*" Kitty shouted.

Happy's eyes went wide. But when she gave a silent hand signal, her troops fell in line behind me.

"*Poshevelivaysya*." Kitty waved the gun at us.

Happy smiled. "She speaks Russian."

Of course she does. I didn't need Happy to translate. It was obvious from Kitty's tone and threatening body language that she meant for us to pose as her prisoners. I hoped to heaven her plan worked. I quickened my pace. Happy hung back and took up the rear.

Kitty marched us up the hall and past the first guard. The second guard stepped in front of her and barked something in Russian. Never breaking eye contact, Kitty responded in kind. He shrugged, stepped back against the wall, and let us pass. We followed Kitty to the front entrance. At the front desk, another armed guard called out to us. "*Octahobka*."

Kitty jabbed the gun into Happy's back and pushed her forward. Happy tightened her lips but didn't say a word. Poppy squirmed in my arms until I sat her on the floor. Kitty spoke to the guard in Russian. The guard replied and then held out his hand and wiggled his fingers at her. She turned and whispered, "He wants to see my orders."

Like a whirling dervish, she whipped around and brought a black boot to the side of his head. "I'll show you my orders." She did a butterfly kick and hit the other side of his head. He fell to the floor in a heap. "Come on." She beckoned to us with the gun. "Let's get out of here."

The fallen guard yelled something and several more guards appeared from the office behind the reception desk.

"*Der'mo*," Kitty hissed.

"*Suka blyad*." Happy joined in the cursing and then ran full bore at the guards.

The rest of the women—and Poppy—joined the charge.

Poppy growled and tore at the hem of the trousers of one of the guards. He kicked and pointed his rifle at her. I lunged at him and knocked him to the ground. Poppy bit his hand, and he let go of the rifle. I grabbed it. He rolled over and made to get up. Poppy slashed his wrist with the diamond on her collar. Howling, he grabbed his bleeding wrist and fell back to the floor.

When I looked up, another guard had his bayonet pointed straight at me. He was picking up speed. I stumbled backwards and tripped over the fallen guard. The bayonet kept coming. It was inches from my chest. A black boot flew past my face and hit the bayonet. Another black boot zipped past and landed on the guard's nose. Blood spurted everywhere. The guard held his nose with both hands and stumbled backwards.

Across the foyer, Happy engaged in hand-to-hand combat with a third guard. She delivered a one-two punch to his jaw, and he dropped like a sack of potatoes. Wasting no time, she snatched his rifle from the floor and smashed the butt into his skull. Blimey. I was beginning to see why it was called the Women's Battalion of Death. I shuddered and made a mental note never to cross Happy.

"Come on!" With Poppy close on her heels, Kitty made for the exit. The rest of us followed.

Outside, a cold wind strafed my legs. Bare feet and a flimsy tunic were no match for early March in Moscow. Shivering, Happy and I said our goodbyes and promised to keep in touch.

"You can contact me at Novodevichy Convent." She squeezed my hand. "Tell Mother Superior you need me, and I'll come."

I nodded. "Thank you."

Kitty bustled me off into a taxi—another miracle. The girl was a wonder. Once we were inside the motorcar, Kitty took my hand between hers and rubbed my freezing fingers. "Whatever were you thinking, Aunt Fiona?"

"I didn't go willingly," I said between chattering teeth.

"Fredricks kidnapped you?" Her eyes widened. "Good." She nodded once. "That's what we'll tell Uncle Blinker."

"No, that's not what I meant." *Curses.* Uncle Blinker, aka Captain Hall, aka my boss. Or should I say *former* boss since, surely, I'd been sacked?

"Yes." She squeezed my hand. "Yes, it is." She gazed directly into my eyes. "You were kidnapped by that devil Fredrick Fredricks. He forcibly brought you to Moscow, where he... he..." she stammered.

"Abandoned me." I averted her gaze.

"Took advantage of you?" she asked. "Used you as a pawn in his talks with the Germans? Fed you to the Bolsheviks?" She squinted at me. "We need a compelling story to get you out of this one."

"Left me for dead?" I suggested.

"Left you for dead," Kitty repeated.

Poppy yipped.

"He might as well have." He'd lured me to Moscow and abandoned me to the Bolsheviks, no thanks to Natasha, aka Countess Brasova. What happened to Natasha? Did she get out? And what about Peggy Hull? I shuddered. I was blessed lucky to be alive. "Thank you, my dear." I patted her hand. "Thank you for rescuing me."

"You'd do the same for me." She smiled. "Right, Poppy-poo?" The pup licked her face.

"I'd do the same for Poppy." I patted the pup and adjusted the bow on her topknot.

"How did you find me?" If she'd broken into my flat, she must have found the letter. My cheeks warmed.

"Fredricks's letter." She narrowed her brows and gave me a disapproving look. "A friend from boarding school." She clasped her hands together as if in prayer. "And Poppy's expert snout." She kissed the pup on said snout.

Disgusting.

"Does the War Office know..." My voice trailed off. What in heaven's name *was* I thinking? I stared down at my hands. I'd worked so hard to be taken seriously as an agent. And now I'd ruined everything. My career. My chances at a normal life with Archie. Archie. Good heavens. What would I tell him?

Kitty eyed the taxi driver. "We're almost there."

"Where?" In my gratitude for being rescued, I hadn't thought to ask where we were going.

The taxi pulled up in front of a brick building. Was Kitty renting a flat? She'd mentioned a friend from boarding school. "Are you staying with your friend from school?"

She shook her head. "This is the British consulate."

The corner of my lip turned up involuntarily. I'd been to British embassies and consulates in six countries now, including Egypt, and this was the most pathetic. There wasn't even a plaque at the entrance.

Good heavens. *What's he doing here?* My stomach flipped. Lieutenant Archie Somersby leaned against the building smoking one of those dreadful Kenilworth cigarettes.

Does Archie know about the letter? The letter from Fredricks? Where the cad invited me to join him at the Metropol Hotel if I changed my mind about marrying Archie. I put my face in my hands. The letter in which Fredricks had promised me the world.

6

THE BRITISH CONSULATE

Archie dropped his cigarette and ground it out under the toe of one of his polished brogues. "Better find her some clothes," he said without even looking at me. Wordlessly, he led us up two flights of stairs.

The consulate was a dusty flat in a dreary building on a Moscow backstreet. Sparsely furnished with peeling paint and scratched wood floors, it looked more like a tenement than an official embassy. And judging by the odd collection of men hunched over the table in the center of the room, I suspected it was a secret MI5 headquarters. Embassies had staff and secretaries and fresh wallpaper. They stood proudly on main avenues. They weren't smokey backroom flats in dilapidated buildings off nondescript alleys.

Archie's presence added credence to my hypothesis. With every passing assignment, I became more convinced he wasn't actually working for Captain Hall and the War Office but for MI5 and the British Secret Service.

"Good lord." Clifford rushed to my side. "What happened to you? You look like something the cat dragged in." He reached out to put a hand on my arm but thought better of it. I didn't blame him. Who knew what critters I'd acquired in that filthy jail? Linebacker nurse scrubbings with lye soap aside. "Thank God you're alright."

What was Clifford doing here? Captain Hall probably insisted he chaperone Kitty, as if she needed one.

"Good to see you, too, Clifford dear." After my ordeal in jail and then that horrible hospital storage room, I wasn't as embarrassed about being seen wearing only a loose-fitting tunic as I should have been. With no wig, my unwashed porcupine hair sticking out in all directions, smelling like a hen house, and barefoot, I'm sure I looked a sight. "Does this place have a bathtub? I could use a good soak."

"You are a tad ripe, old bean." Clifford waved his hand in front of his nose and chuckled.

When I glanced over at the table, I caught Archie staring at me. My cheeks burned. He still had that adorable lock of chestnut hair falling down his forehead and those beautiful green eyes. Why didn't I just marry him when he'd asked? Why had I told him to wait until after the war? If only I'd accepted his proposal, none of this would have happened. I looked away. Of all people, I hated him seeing me like this.

"Let's get you cleaned up." Kitty led me by the arm. "Then I'll brief you on your assignment."

"Assignment?" I wasn't fired? "What about my clothes?" By now, the Metropol Hotel staff were probably wearing them. *Sigh.* My favorite lavender cloche hat. And that new violet gabardine dress I'd splurged on at Harrods.

"I brought clothes." Kitty took me into the bathroom and shut the door.

I hoped she didn't expect me to wear pink frilly numbers like hers. At this point, anything would be better than this nasty burlap sack. I tugged at the tunic, eager for Kitty to leave me so I could rip the stinking thing off my irritated skin.

She turned on the tap in the bathtub. When she whispered, I realized the running water was not just for my bath but also to camouflage her voice. "Your assignment is to go under cover as a nanny in the house of Victor Volodarsky, also known as Iron Victor, the head of the Cheka secret police, known here as Vcheka."

Crikey. Iron Victor. The head of the Cheka secret police. I stood there blinking at her. Not just any assignment. A deuced dangerous one.

"Your mission is crucial to the war effort and highly classified. It's imperative that Russia stay the course and protect the Eastern Front." Kitty laid a small towel across the edge of the tub. "If they surrender to Germany, we'll be next."

England surrender to Germany. I shuddered. Never. It was impossible to imagine. Even more impossible was the weight of the future on my narrow shoulders. Fiona Figg, file clerk and newly minted British agent on a crucial assignment. I hoped to heaven I was up to the task. I'd better be. My redemption was at stake.

"The details are in a file folder from Uncle Blinker." She took a step toward me. "I have your disguise and papers. Your cover alias is Holly Heatherfield."

"Papers?" I shivered. The stone floor was cold on my bare feet. I could hardly wait to strip off my tunic and climb into the steaming bathtub.

"You're a British nanny joining your sister who just married a soldier in the Red Army. That way I can visit you if necessary."

Red Army. White Army. Bolsheviks. Tsarists. Deuced confusing situation with so many factions jockeying for power. I looked longingly at my bath.

"Seems Iron Victor likes the idea of a British woman cleaning his children's bottoms." She raised her eyebrows. "Your references are in the file folder."

"Cleaning bottoms." It was a lot to take in, especially with my own bare bum hanging out of a burlap tunic.

She turned off the tap. "While you bathe, I'll fetch your clothes." The tub was full, so apparently the briefing was over for now.

"And my wig?" I thought of the poor abused strawberry-blonde bob she'd had tucked into her back pocket. "Any way to recover my things from the Metropol?"

"I'm on it." She pointed to the tub. "Wash up and then we'll get you some food and put you to bed. Your assignment starts first thing tomorrow." She lowered her voice. "Russia signed the treaty with Germany and the War Office needs intel on the best way to undermine the Bolshevik government."

"Undermine the government." I'd never undermined a government before.

"The men and I are working on an operation to overthrow the Bolsheviks and get Russia back on our side. But we need to know what's going on with Iron Victor. He's key."

"The men attack from the outside while I get inside, is that it?" I asked.

"Precisely." She waved me into the tub. "Get to it. I'll fill you in on the details later."

I nodded.

She pulled a wrapped square from a hidden pocket in her sleek black jumpsuit. "A present." She held it out to me.

"What's this?" I took it. "A bar of soap."

"Formerly Bouquet de Catherine." She raised her eyebrows. "Before the Soviets nationalized soap production. Now it's called No. 1."

"Just as long as it's not lye." I unwrapped the soap and sniffed. Lovely.

Once she'd left the bathroom, I gladly stripped off the dirty tunic and stepped into the warm water. *Ahhh.* Heavenly. I'd never wanted—or needed—a bath so badly in my life. I welcomed the scented soap. I couldn't distinguish the fragrance. Was it some combination of jasmine, rose, vanilla, and wet wood? Even after I'd scrubbed with the perfumed soap, I still smelled the lingering scent of fear. It would be a while before I could wash away the terror of my stint in a Russian jail.

Soaking was conducive to cogitating. As I lay in the bath, I reviewed the chaotic state of my life and tried to formulate a way forward that wouldn't result in too much egg on my face. Thankfully, Kitty had covered for me with Captain Hall. I'd doubted her in the past, but she was a good girl and a loyal partner. Thanks to her, I still had my job. And a new assignment. Obviously, the War Office believed the way to undermine the Bolsheviks and overthrow the government lay with the secret police. From what I'd seen, the Cheka were the enforcers of the Bolshevik government. Without them—and the terror they engendered—the government would be toothless.

Politics made my head spin. But it was better than agonizing about my former almost-fiancé on the other side of the bathroom door. Or that rotter Fredrick Fredricks, who had lured me here and then abandoned me. The whole ordeal was humiliating to say the least.

A quick rap on the door gave me little warning before Kitty barged in. I curled up in a ball and wrapped my arms around my knees.

"Your clothes." Kitty sat a suitcase on the floor next to the bathtub. Not just any suitcase. *My* suitcase.

"How did you get that?" I leaned over the edge of the tub for a better look.

"I have connections." Kitty flashed a smug smile. "Okay. My school friend Olga's brother's pal's cousin works as a bellboy at the Metropol."

I gave up following the chain of relations. "Thank you." I couldn't wait to get back into my own clothes.

"Hurry and get dressed." Kitty reached for the doorknob. "We have a lot to go over before tomorrow." Who made her the boss? I supposed it was a small price to pay to have my job back.

When I heard the door shut, I hopped out of the bath, grabbed the nearest—should I say only—towel, and dried off. I balanced my suitcase on the top of the toilet and snapped open its locks. Oh, my brown tweed skirt with bespoke pockets especially designed for my spy paraphernalia. Filled with glee, I plucked it up and hugged it to my chest. And my cream silk blouse. I dropped my skirt and picked up my lavender cloche. Putting on clean knickers and my own skirt and blouse was like slipping back into my skin. Ahh. I felt like myself again. And just in time to transform into Holly Heatherfield, nifty nanny and bottom cleaner.

Whoever had packed my suitcase had stuffed my blonde bob in between my practical Oxfords. I swallowed my curses and reminded myself I was lucky to have any wig, let alone my favorite. *Happy not complain.* I tugged it on and then went to the mirror. Even with the bobbed wig, I looked like my uncle Frank playing dress-up. If only I had some rouge and eye kohl. I rummaged through my case to see if Kitty's friend's brother's so-and-so had included my toiletries bag.

More important than impressing a current fiancé was impressing a former one.

I fixed my hair and face as best as I could under the circumstances, and then listened at the bathroom door. The men were talking in hushed voices. I couldn't hear what they said, but their tone was serious. I took a deep breath and twisted the doorknob. When I stepped out of the bathroom, all heads turned, and all eyes were on me. Ignoring my burning cheeks, I headed toward the table. Strictly professional. I glanced at Archie and immediately regretted it. He blushed, and my pulse quickened. *We're work colleagues, nothing more.*

Clifford gave me a broad smile. But the other men, the strangers, clammed up and stared at me with distrust.

"It's okay," Archie said. "She's one of us."

"And who is us?" I tried to sound nonchalant as I stared down at the map spread out on the table.

"Special agent Fiona Figg." Archie introduced me around to the men, who one by one nodded or smiled my way.

With his thick wavy hair and bow tie, the young British ambassador Sir Robert Bruce Hamilton Lockhart looked like a public schoolboy. Sidney Reilly was a handsome, well-dressed man who had the look of someone who always got what he wanted. Yet, with his three-piece suit, starched white collar, and pince-nez glasses, he looked more like a bookkeeper than a spymaster. No doubt the cane he carried held a sword blade in one end and a secret codebook in the other. Boris Savinkov, the Russian military man, was as excitable and bloodthirsty as a wire-haired terrier on the scent of a fox.

Kitty twirled around, holding Poppy in her arms, cooing like a ninny. As night becomes day, she'd changed from her sleek foot-fighting outfit into a frilly pink frock. I preferred the night-fighting Kitty to the silly frilly daytime Kitty. But I had to admire her performance.

I suspected both extremes were artifice and I had yet to meet the real Kitty Lane.

Sir Robert Lockhart went back to pointing at the map in the center of the table. It was a map of Moscow with a hand-drawn inlay of the layout of the Kremlin. Sir Robert poked a finger at a domed building in the center of the Kremlin. "This is the Kremlin Senate. Lenin will have his study and private residence on the third floor." He tapped another building. "This is the Kremlin Armory."

I moved closer to get a better look.

Never taking his eyes off me, Sidney Reilly replaced the map of Moscow and the Kremlin with an architectural sketch of the inside of a building. As he rolled up one map and unfurled another, I got a strong whiff of bergamot. Did the man bathe in the stuff? "We have it from a reliable source that the Bolshevik government is moving to Moscow on 10 March." He tapped at the map like a chicken pecking at corn. "Not 11 March like they've publicly announced."

Good heavens—10 March. That was the second date on the back of Fredricks's matchbox. *10-03. 10-03 P-M.* Petrograd to Moscow. He'd written down the date of the Bolsheviks' move from Petrograd to Moscow. The last notation was ??-?? WRD. The question marks meant date unknown—or not yet known. What was WRD? *Withdraw Russian Defense. Wet Road Detour. Wicked Rotten Duke.* So far, I'd been one step behind Fredricks. I had to figure out a way to get ahead of him and get back on a firm footing with the War Office.

Using both hands, Sidney Reilly flattened the blueprint. "We will pose as removal men and enter the building here." He drummed a back entrance with his finger. "We'll take advantage of the turmoil..." The heady scent of his cologne was overpowering. He wasn't going to sneak up on anyone smelling like that.

"To pop Lenin," the Russian military man said, a broad smile slicing his thin face.

Blimey. They planned to assassinate the leader of the Soviet government. What was my part in all of this? From the nursery, was I supposed to sabotage Iron Victor and the secret police?

"Lenin and any of his *associates*," Archie narrowed his eyes and glared at me, "who get in our way." His steely gaze cut right through me. The way he'd said associates, I knew exactly who he meant.

A shiver ran up my spine.

He planned to kill Fredrick Fredricks.

7

HOLLY HEATHERFIELD

That evening, while everyone was out preparing for the mission, I got to rest on a sofa at the consulate. I had one night to shed the stench of jail, get some color back in my cheeks, and shrink the dark circles under my eyes. Exhausted, I spent the entire evening lounging and studying the file folder Kitty had given me.

Iron Victor had been a revolutionary since adolescence. He'd been in and out of prison, exiled to Siberia, and tortured, and still he believed. Last year, after the October revolution, he was freed from jail. Lenin appointed him head of the Cheka, secret police, and charged him with putting down counter-revolution. He was ruthless and cunning, inciting fear and using it to control tsarists into submission. And when fear didn't work, he resorted to extermination.

Had I read that correctly? Extermination? As in insects? And here I was, a fly about to enter the spider's web.

* * *

Early the next morning, Kitty helped me prepare to become Holly the gifted governess. She'd brought a plain gray skirt with a matching gray woolen jacket. Underneath, I wore a white blouse with a high starched collar. Instead of my favorite strawberry-blonde bob, we went for something a bit more old-fashioned: a mousy-brown chignon. Not my favorite, but it was effective. By the time we finished, I looked like a prudish spinster destined to spend the rest of her life reading about romance instead of actually experiencing it.

"Aunt Fiona, can I ask you something?" Kitty straightened my collar.

I squinted at her. She'd never asked to ask something before. "Alright."

"Why don't you want to marry Archie?" She leveled her gaze. "He seems a decent sort. At least better than Fredrick Fredricks."

My cheeks warmed at the mention of Fredricks. How I wished she didn't know I'd run after him. Who else knew? Mortified, I closed my eyes. "I only asked to wait until after the war." I opened my eyes and returned her gaze. "Is that so unreasonable?"

"If you love each other, why wait?" She unpinned the lace from an already dowdy bucket hat. "Or don't you love him?"

I stared down at my lisle gloves. "How can you tell if you love someone?" I bit my lip. This wasn't exactly an appropriate conversation for spy masters. Moreover, I was seven years older than Kitty and had been married before, for pity's sake.

"I wouldn't know." Kitty adjusted my wig and tucked up a stray hair. "All I know is you should stay away from Fredrick Fredricks. He's dangerous."

"Yes, well..." In my experience, Fredricks was no more dangerous than any other man committed to his cause. He might be my enemy, but he'd treated me with more respect than some

of my friends. "You have to admit, he's got a certain charisma."
Indeed, he was annoyingly charming.

"It's all an act." Kitty held her hand in front of her mouth and
giggled. "A performance." She squealed and batted her lashes.
"Artifice designed to open the doors of society so he can carry out
his nefarious schemes." She plucked Poppy from the floor and
twirled her around. "Right, Poppy-poo?" Kissing the pup's flat
nose, she giggled some more. She sat Poppy back on the floor and
stood up straight. "See, an act."

Alright. She'd fooled me and everyone else with her silly
schoolgirl act.

"And you're disguised as a nanny." She stuffed the ugly hat on
top of my wig. "You've passed as a man, for Pete's sake. A
performance."

A hatpin pricked my ear. "Ouch!" I gave her a nasty look. "No
need to stab me."

"The best spies are flirts." She continued fussing with my hat.
"It comes with the territory."

"Anything for king and country," I said sarcastically. "You
think marrying Archie is my patriotic duty?"

She laughed. Not her usual schoolgirl giggle, but a real laugh.
"Marriage is used by men to force women into servitude."

"So, I shouldn't marry Archie?" I was confused. Hadn't she
just told me to marry him? Or did she think that I should be
forced into servitude?

"If that's what it takes to keep you from throwing yourself at
Fredrick Fredricks, then yes, you should marry Archie." Her eyes
were hard. Nothing like a silly schoolgirl.

"Throwing myself." I sniffed. I was hardly *throwing* myself.

"Look." She took me by the shoulders. "Your knickers are in
such a twist you won't be able to think straight until you bed—"

"Good heavens!" I jerked out of her grip. Impertinent girl. "That's no way for a young lady to talk."

She scoffed. "I'm old enough to know that lust is not the same as love."

Lust. How could she say such a thing? Speechless, I stood staring at her. Who was this girl? Certainly not the sweet innocent I'd taken her for when I'd met her four months ago.

"If you're such a prude that you can't abide hanky-panky without marriage, then you'd best get married." She tugged on the bottom of my jacket with such force that I almost toppled over.

"I'm not a prude." I slipped on my practical Oxfords and examined myself in the mirror. A prim and proper English governess, yes. But not a prude. "No more indecent talk. We've got a mission to complete." I, for one, wanted to complete the mission, get out of this godforsaken country, and away from both Fredrick Fredricks and Archie Somersby.

Speaking of Fredricks, where was the bounder?

* * *

Carrying my strategically packed nanny's valise, I arrived on Iron Victor's doorstep. Ready to assume the duties of a live-in governess and spy, I took a deep breath and knocked. A middle-aged woman answered the door. Her hair was pulled back so tight it stretched her forehead into a shiny dome, and the dark circles under her eyes looked like sunken stones. She wore a long black dress with a white pinafore apron.

"I'm Holly Heatherfield, the new governess." I showed her my identity papers. She nodded as she led me inside.

The low wooden gridded ceiling and the brown-and-gold checkered floor tiles arranged in boxy cross patterns made me feel like I was inside a waffle press. The only relief came from an oval window above the entrance that admitted a ray of light. The housemaid glided across the foyer toward a curved staircase with an ornately carved wooden banister.

"I just arrived from London." I trotted to keep up with her. "My younger sister lives here. I got this post to be close to her."

She nodded again but didn't say a word. She led me up a grand marble staircase, glancing back as I nattered on, but her stony expression never changed. She stopped in front of a door and gestured for me to go inside. I was beginning to suspect that she didn't speak English.

"The nursery?" I asked in my limited Russian. Or at least that is what I hoped I'd asked.

Her hard face broke into a smile. A floodgate opened and she spoke a mile a minute. I didn't understand a word. Except *"deti."* Children. My Russian was limited to what I had memorized from the dictionary, which worked better on paper than in practice.

The nursery was bright, with large windows and colorful green and orange wallpaper. In the center of the room, in the middle of a Persian carpet, three children sat cross-legged, playing a game. The oldest looked to be about ten and the youngest was probably four or five. Two boys, and a girl, who was giving her younger brothers instructions and grabbing playing pieces from their hands—the girl was obviously in charge. All three had sandy brown hair, light brown eyes, and thin lips. The boys were wearing matching sailor suits and the girl wore a white dress.

The housemaid said something to them. They stopped their game and stared up at me.

"Good morning, children," I said in what I hoped was a welcoming but firm tone. "I'm Miss Heatherfield, your new governess."

The girl jumped up and came over to me. She held out her small hand. "Enchanted to meet you."

I took her hand. "The pleasure is mine." I smiled down at her.

"My name is Anna." She turned back to her brothers and barked something at them. They both sprang up from the rug and dashed over to me.

"I am Vitya." The tallest boy held out his hand to me.

"Glad to meet you, Vitya."

"I am Luka." The smaller boy imitated his older brother.

"Nice to know you, Luka." I was glad I was wearing my gloves to protect from whatever creepy crawlies were lurking on those grubby little hands.

The housemaid left and shut the door. A panic rose in my throat. I was trapped with three children. What did I know of children? I'd been unable to have any of my own. A familiar ache took up residence in my chest. I suspected that was the real reason Andrew had left me. Yes, his secretary, Nancy, the husband-stealing tart, was attractive. But she was also fertile and gave him the son he'd always wanted. Another familiar pang struck my heart. This time a pang of guilt. I'd promised Andrew on his deathbed that I'd look out for his young son. But my life of espionage left little time for anything else, especially someone else's son. Last time I'd seen him, he was just a baby. He must be almost a year old now.

For the rest of the morning, I tidied the nursery, rehearsed the alphabet, and sang songs with the children. Anna filled me in on their regular schedule, her parents' expectations, and what had happened to their last English nanny. I shuddered as she excitedly recounted in gory detail how the poor young woman was taken to prison and then shot by a firing squad for spying. Anna had assured me that the woman wasn't a spy but a champion chess player who could beat even the men. That was why they'd killed her. Crikey. I'd better watch my step. True. I wasn't a crack chess player. But I was a spy.

In the late afternoon, the housemaid delivered the children's supper of roasted potatoes and charred meat. My stomach growled, reminding me that I hadn't eaten. Anna informed me the governess always ate with them, and they ate early on Mondays when her mother went out to play bridge. Sitting with three children around the little table, in a chair that was several sizes too small, I felt like I was playing at having a tea party. The meal was simple but satisfying. Anna told me that the meat was lamb from her grandparents' farm. I smiled. I too had spent time on my grandparents' farm as a girl. Over dinner, we exchanged stories of feeding and grooming animals. I didn't tell her that I spent most of my time hiding in the hay loft reading Sherlock Holmes stories.

After supper, I went to the bookshelf and at the boys' request selected *The Wonderful Wizard of Oz* as our bedtime reading. As I read aloud Dorothy's adventures in the Emerald City, I wondered whether I would meet Mr. and Mrs. Volodarsky or spend the next month locked up in this nursery. Another wave of panic hit me. The housemaid always shut the door to the nursery on her way out. I hadn't stepped foot outside the room and neither had the children. What if we were locked up in here? Like Dorothy, I needed an escape plan. As soon as the children were asleep, I would go exploring. Hopefully, as long as I avoided the chess board, I wouldn't meet the same end as the last governess. The boys clapped with glee when I read the part about the jungle monkeys with bird-like feathered wings.

A slight rap on the door was followed by a whirlwind of silky fabrics entering the room. An attractive woman whooshed in, and all three children ran to greet her. Laughing, she enveloped them in her long arms. When she spoke, she sounded like a honeybee

buzzing, soft and melodious. She glanced over and beckoned to
me. I heeded her gesture but kept out of arm's reach. Smiling, she
said something to me in Russian. Blast. Why wasn't my brain fast
enough to look up the words in my memory's dictionary and then
transliterate? Learning vocabulary was one thing. Learning a
living language, quite another. When I didn't respond, she turned
to her daughter. Anna was only too happy to act as our inter-
preter. The way she took control of her mother, I was beginning
to think that Anna ran the place.

"Mama apologizes for not meeting you earlier." Anna's tone
was serious and efficient. "She and Papa just returned from
important business in Brest-Litovsk."

Brest-Litovsk. I nodded. That was where the treaty negotiations took place. Did she know Fredricks? No doubt he knew her.
The blackguard seemed to know everyone.

"Mama and Papa invite you to join them in the library in an
hour." Anna looked from me to her mother and back again. "Will
you accept?"

"Of course." I smiled politely. "I would be delighted."

"They look forward to interviewing you then." Anna took her
mother's hand and then took mine, as if forming a human chain.
Her small hand in mine should have been reassuring. Instead, it
was clear she intended to take both her mother and me in hand.

"Interview?" I asked, trying to hide my trepidation. Was it a
translation error? If Anna noticed my palms had broken out in a
cold sweat, she didn't let on.

"Papa is very strict in his expectations." She flashed a smug
smile.

If I weren't so anxious about my upcoming interview with
Iron Victor, I'd admire the girl's language skills, not to mention
her maturity.

Mrs. Volodarsky kissed each child in turn, patted the boys on the head, and then whispered something to Anna.

"*Da*, Mama," Anna said, nodding.

When their mother had left the room, I turned to Anna. "What did she say?"

"I'm to help you put the boys to bed and then deliver you to the library." Her tone was matter-of-fact. "Come on, boys." She held out a hand to each of them. Taking them in hand now, too.

"You're very grown up." She was mature beyond her years. A veritable force of nature.

"Papa is always working. And Mama is busy entertaining the bosses." Anna tugged on her brothers' hands. "It's up to me to keep the household running and the boys out from under foot," she said, no doubt reciting what she'd been told.

"And a very good job you do, too." I nodded once for emphasis.

"Thank you." Anna led the boys to their beds. "I told Mama that we didn't need a governess. I can read and write and take care of my brothers."

"Yes, I'm sure you can." I swallowed. A niggling at the back of my brain told me this job might be more difficult than I'd imagined. And that was saying something.

8

THE INTERVIEW

With no small amount of trepidation, I followed Anna down the stairs and into the library, where her parents were waiting. I could feel the blood pumping in my throat. From what I'd heard about Iron Victor, he wasn't a man to trifle with and he didn't suffer fools. I had to put my best foot forward to impress him. And a rather large and ungainly foot it was.

Anna pulled the heavy wooden door open, and I stepped inside. Golly. I'd never seen so many books in one room. Yes, it was a library. But usually in posh houses, libraries were in name only. These were not leather-bound books for show but well-used books. Here, bookshelves went from floor to ceiling on every wall but one. The one with the fireplace. All the way up to the ceiling. Attached to each shelf was a wooden ladder on wheels that could move back and forth. The sheer number of books was dizzying.

The fireplace was gorgeous, with inlaid turquoise and tan tile-work and an ornately carved wooden hearth and hood that extended all the way to the ceiling. The wooden mantelpiece depicted what looked like a hunting scene with men on horse-back. Above the mantel hung a large, brightly colored painting. If you stared at it long enough—as if looking through water at a world turned sideways—you could make out buildings and trees. The wall surrounding the fireplace had wood panels on the bottom half and cheerful deep blue wallpaper with an inlaid fern design on the top half. All very cozy.

I waited in the doorway until Mrs. V called me inside. Or at least I think she did. She looked in my direction, said something, and waved. Whatever she said next sent Anna scurrying back to the nursery.

Iron Victor sat in a high-backed chair, reading a newspaper and smoking a thin cigar. I crossed the room. He ignored me, which wasn't necessarily bad. It was the *way* he ignored me, as if he'd thrown up an iron curtain around his chair. Not to make himself invisible. But to enshrine his power over me. The power to acknowledge me or ignore me. The power to swat or disregard a pesky insect buzzing around him.

The man had a high forehead topped with thick black hair. His full mustache and beard were also black. The mustache was waxed and turned up into points, while the beard curled under his chin. The ghastly thing. His brows were heavy and arched. His long sharp nose split his face evenly. As he read his newspaper, his eyes wore a perpetual squint. If his features weren't so hard and his gaze so terrifying, he'd be a handsome man. Still, he was a small man—what he lacked in stature, he made up for in intensity. Maybe I was prejudiced by his file, but even relaxing in his own library, he exuded severity.

Sitting near the fireplace, I glanced around the space, taking it all in. Perhaps I would see something worth reporting to the War Office. A wooden desk caught my eye. The kind of desk with several drawers for files and important papers. The desk straddled one whole corner of the room. Atop the desk was a pretty stained-glass lamp and a gold inkwell and pen set.

I sat erect on my overstuffed chair and waited. A lively tune played on the phonograph. Like Wassily Kandinsky, the composer was fond of mad tubas. Mrs. V smiled but said nothing. She'd given up trying to communicate with me. It was going to be a deuced awkward interview.

When the recording ended, Iron Victor finally broke the silence. "Do you read Gorky, Miss Heatherfield?" He didn't look up from his paper. His English was impeccable. "Silence is terrible and torturous to only those who have no more to say, but, to those who have not started to speak—to them silence is simple and light." He snapped his newspaper shut. "Which are you, Miss Heatherfield?"

"I beg your pardon, sir?" My head was spinning.

"Nothing more to say or have you not yet started to speak?" He glowered over at me. "You're too young and... naïve to have nothing more to say." He shrugged and went back to his paper.

What made him think I was naïve? At twenty-five, I wasn't so young. "If I may ask, where did you learn English?" I folded my hands in my lap to keep from leaping up and running away. "You speak beautifully."

"Englishmen are self-assured because they think they know everything, and everything is fully knowable." He paused. "Russians are self-assured because they know they know nothing... because nothing is fully knowable."

Good grief. Did the man always talk in riddles? I sat there blinking like an idiot. And not Dostoevsky's idiot.

"Certainly, you've read Tolstoy, Miss Heatherfield?" His voice was indignant. "Excusing his Christian pacifism, he's got some redeeming virtues."

"Yes, sir... of course. All happy families are alike," I stammered. "Each unhappy family is unhappy in its own way?" It came out like a question.

"Everyone knows the opening line to *Anna Karenina*." He stood up. Although he was shorter than me, his commanding voice made him seem bigger. "How can you teach my children unless you first teach yourself?"

He had a point.

"Russian literature and art are the best in the world. Do you know why?"

Because we were in Russia? And Iron Victor was Russian? And a nationalist to boot?

"I'll tell you why." He towered over me—only because I was still seated—and jabbed the air with his cigarillo. Lingering under the foul stench of smoke was the smell of a swamp on a hot day. "Russians are self-reflective, self-aware, and self-deprecating." Sounded more like self-aggrandizement. "Dostoevsky, Tolstoy, Pushkin." With every name another jab. "Philosopher-poets. They don't just write literature. They question its very existence. Nothing is sacred." He took a deep draw off his cigarillo. "We Russians question everything. The irreverence of Gogol. Even Chekov's clinical approach to ordinary virtues—"

"I'm an educated Englishwoman, of course I'm familiar—"

He cut me off. Pointing at the painting over the fireplace, he continued my lesson. "Wassily Kandinsky's paintings throw down the gauntlet."

Kandinsky. The chap from the magazine. I thought I'd recognized the style. The mad tuba.

"Which of your English painters challenge us to question everything we see?" He puffed his cigar and blew out a plume of smoke at me.

Truth be told, the only English artist who came to mind was Sidney Paget, the illustrator of the Sherlock Holmes stories. "Well, um," I stammered.

"I thought so." He gave me a smug look.

I'd had quite enough of his lecture. "If you want your children well educated in Russian literature, why not hire a Russian governess?"

He scoffed. "Only the connoisseur can judge what is best." He smirked. "Isn't that what your own John Stuart Mill maintains?" Turning on his heels, he went back to his throne. "I want my children to learn about your culture and your literature so they will truly appreciate the superiority of our own."

Well, I never... "And what if, after sampling ours, they decide yours is *not* the best?"

"Then my hat is off to you for—how did your Reverend Jonathan Swift say it—making a silk purse out of a sow's ear."

If we English were so bad, why did he keep quoting my countrymen?

With the drama of a stage conductor, he flipped his newspaper open and disappeared back into its pages.

I took that as my cue. I'd been hired... and dismissed for the evening.

"Miss Heatherfield." Iron Victor folded down the top section of his paper like a flap. "Please watch over our Anna." He glanced over at his wife. "She has a bad habit of sleepwalking."

"Sleepwalking." I bobbed a quick curtsey. "Yes, sir."

"And Miss Heatherfield, can you put the phonograph record on again?" He pointed to a large cabinet. "You would do well to listen to our Stravinsky, too."

"Yes, sir." I went to the phonograph cabinet and lifted the lid. The recording was called "The Fox." More like the fox in the henhouse by my accounts. I lifted the heavy arm and put it down gently on the edge of the record. When I turned back, Iron Victor was buried in his newspaper again. I nodded to Mrs. V, who had watched the entire inquisition over the edge of a martini glass. Quickly, I made my escape.

Outside the library, the house was dark and quiet. An eerie emptiness followed me up the stairs. Carefully, I opened the door and tiptoed into the nursery. It was a relief to be back. The boys were asleep. Anna was tucked in her bed reading a book. A girl after my own heart.

"Anna, dear," I said gently. "Shouldn't you turn out the light and go to sleep?" As I crossed the room, I memorized the layout in case I had to creep out in the dark or tackle a sleepwalking Anna.

"Please, Miss Heatherfield." Her knuckles white from clutching the book, she glanced up at me with pleading eyes. "May I finish this chapter?"

"Very well." I knew what it was like to be in the grip of a good book, especially a good mystery.

I retired to my small bedroom, which was separated from the nursery by a door. Thank goodness. The door had no lock, but at least I could get a moment's privacy.

Rather than get ready for bed, I sat fully clothed on the edge of my bed and watched the door. When the light disappeared from the nursery, I waited until I was sure the children would be asleep. Before exiting my room, I did a quick inventory of the spy paraphernalia in my pockets. Since my own implements were confiscated when I was arrested, Kitty had lent me her lockpick set. And, of course, I had a notebook and pencil, as always. My memory was good, but sometimes it was best to supplement it with good notes. As I crept out of my room and across the nursery, I wished I had Mata Hari's gun. Unfortunately, Kitty, the little minx, hadn't given it back. I didn't want to be unarmed and run into that scary bloke Iron Victor in the shadows.

The staircase was dark and so was the hallway below. There was barely enough light coming through the oval window above the entrance to illuminate my way. Any darker and I'd resort to my torch. I crept down the stairs and tiptoed across the hall toward the library. I'd settled on the library as my first stop since I'd been there before and knew the lie of the land. Blast. There was still light coming from under the library door. I froze in place. Voices. Men's voices. Were the Volodarskys entertaining at this time of night? Best not get caught sneaking around. Death by firing squad did not appeal to me. I crept back upstairs, across the nursery, and into my own room. I lay back on my bed. My frantic week in Moscow hit me like a ton of bricks. I was completely knackered. No wonder, after my harrowing experiences of the last few days. I closed my eyes. I must have fallen asleep with my clothes on. When I woke up, it was daylight.

I quickly tidied myself and looked in on the children. They were all still asleep. I went back to my room to prepare lesson plans. My cover was only as good as my lessons. Iron Victor wouldn't put up with anything other than the highest performance. The trick would be teaching all three children at once. Anna already spoke perfect English. I could have her read on her own while I gave the boys more rudimentary lessons.

The next morning, after the children woke, bathed, dressed, and had their breakfast, I began the lessons. They were well behaved and didn't fuss. The day passed pleasantly. I rather enjoyed teaching. And the children were a delight, especially Anna. Such a precocious little thing. Since the weather was so cold and dreadful, we spent the entire day in the nursery. Other than the children, the only person I saw was the maid when she delivered the meals. She was not that much older than Anna. And they were friendly. Probably too friendly. As she put the lunch tray on our small table, the maid whispered something to Anna. They both giggled. After the maid left, I approached Anna.

"What was that all about?" I sat next to her in one of the undersized chairs.

"Nothing." Anna gave me a coy smile.

"I'll let you finish your book tonight even if it's past your bedtime." I raised my eyebrows. Might as well teach her bribery at an early age.

A broad smile spread across her face. "Promise you won't tell?"

"Cross my heart." I made an X over my chest.

"Cook is cross with Papa." Anna giggled. "She said if he complains about her cooking again, she's going to poison his borscht."

I narrowed my brows. "There's nothing funny about poison." I'd seen enough poisoning to know.

"She's joking." Anna's eyes went wide. "You don't think she could be serious?"

"Of course not." I passed up the soup just in case.

Evening came and went and I still hadn't stepped foot out of the nursery. How was I going to find out anything useful holed up in the nursery all day?

That night, once the children were sound asleep and well after everyone should have been in bed, I snuck out. Again, there was a light coming from the library. I tiptoed up to the door and listened. Men's voices. I recognized Iron Victor's voice. There were two other men. Their conversation was passionate. A creaking sound from the stairs made me whirl around. A small ghostlike figure floated down the stairs. My breath caught.

Only Anna. What a relief. She must be sleepwalking. I intercepted her on the stairs and guided her back to the nursery. I realized Anna's sleepwalking could be a good excuse for my own nocturnal wandering.

The next day passed very much like the one before. That night again I waited until well after midnight for the household to retire to bed. Again, I snuck out and crept down the stairs. I headed for the library, which seemed to be where Iron Victor entertained his guests.

Holding my breath, I listened at the door. Silence. Had Mr. and Mrs. V retired for the evening? I glanced down and didn't see any light coming from under the library door. Slowly, I pushed the door open a crack and peeked in. I could always say I'd dropped a glove or lost an earring and had come back to fetch it. Or I was looking for a wayward Anna.

The room was dark except for the glowing embers from the fireplace. I stepped inside. Carefully, I shut the door behind me. I pulled the torch from my pocket. On tiptoe, I crossed the room to one of the bookshelves. Shining the torch up and down the shelves, I read off the titles. Mr. and Mrs. V had an impressive library with everything from economics to philosophy, and litera-ture written in several languages. Surprising for the chief of the secret police. I thought of Fredrick Fredricks, with his penchant for weighty tomes.

After I'd inspected the bookshelves, I went to the heavy mahogany desk in the corner. Atop an ink blotter lay a large carved wooden box and its smaller rectangular mate. I laid my torch on the desk and opened the larger box. Inside I found stationery embossed with a seal. Picking up my torch, I took a closer look. The seal was an oval shield with a sword slicing down its middle. Around the sword were wrapped an anvil and sickle. Inside the oval was a big red letter V. For Victor? For Volodarsky? I remembered what Kitty had said. The Russians called the Cheka Vcheka. V for secret police. I'd seen this insignia before. On Fredricks's note.

The smaller box contained writing instruments, very fine pens and pencils. I tried opening the top drawer. Locked. Kneeling in front of the drawer, I took out my lockpick set and got to work. With a bit of pressure from my tiny wrench, the drawer clicked open. I stuffed the lockpick set back into my pocket, grabbed my torch, and shone it inside the drawer. Pulling the drawer further open, I examined its contents. One sealed envelope caught my eye.

The outside of the envelope was marked "OB." I lifted the envelope, slid it out of the drawer, and turned it over in my hands. The other side was marked "DDR." For a moment, I thought it was WRD, the same notation I'd found on the back of Fredricks's matchbox. What did OB stand for in Russian? And what was DDR?

I ran my finger across the lip of the envelope. Could I break the seal without tearing the envelope? More importantly, could I unseal it and then reseal it? I studied the seal. Wax with the same insignia from the stationery. If I warmed it and then lifted it off, perhaps I could rewarm the bottom and reattach it. I made a mental note to add matches or a lighter to my spy paraphernalia.

I took my chances. Holding my breath, I carefully lifted the seal and pried the envelope open. I stopped and listened. Silence. Shining the torch on the envelope, I slid out the contents.

Along with photographs of the royal family, there was one typed page stamped with "OB" in large letters. The page was in Russian, of course. I scanned it, quickly taking a mental snapshot. The names of the royal family stood out—Nicholas Romanov, Alexandra Romanov, their three daughters and their son, Alexei Romanov, heir to the throne. There was also a picture of a fortified mansion. If I wasn't mistaken, the caption read *Ipatiev House in Yekaterinburg*, "House of Special Purpose." If I recalled correctly —and I always did—the countess said the royal family was being held in Tobolsk, not Yekaterinburg. Curious. What in the world was I looking at? Whatever it was involved plans for the royal family.

Typed across the top of every page in the envelope were three words: *директива белой розы*. I closed my eyes and called forth *Hill's Russian-English vest-pocket dictionary*. One letter and word at a time, I raced to transliterate and then translate. The letters and words appeared before my mind's eye. As if I was holding the dictionary in my hands, mentally I flipped through the pages until I found each word. Direkiva. Deloy. Rozy. Directive. White. Rose. Crikey. White Rose Directive. WRD. The notation on Fredricks's matchbox. ??-?? WRD. If I was right, and the other notations were dates, then the White Rose Directive's dates were to be determined. Judging by the contents of this envelope, the White Rose Directive was a plan to move the royal family. But why?

Voices from the hall stopped me in my tracks. My pulse quickened. Were the voices getting closer? The rattle of the doorknob sent me flying under the desk. Panting from fear, I tucked my knees up under my chin and crouched into the smallest ball possible. I closed my eyes and waited to be caught. The purloined envelope was sandwiched between my chest and my thighs. Taking deep breaths, I tried to slow my racing heart. The voices were in the room now. Two men's voices. One I recognized as Iron Victor's. When the lights came on, I saw it lying there on the floor where I'd dropped it. My torch. Good heavens. And the top drawer of the desk was still open. Silently setting the envelope aside, I leaned forward, rolling myself onto hands and knees, and then carefully reached out my arm for the torch. Curses. It was just out of reach. I held my breath and jutted my arm out and grabbed it. Torch in hand, I froze and again waited to be caught... and then executed.

The men's voices weren't getting closer. I surmised Iron Victor and his guest were sitting near the fireplace. The embers would still be emitting some heat. I listened for a few seconds and then reached up and touched the drawer. Slowly, I applied pressure.

The drawer creaked and the men's voices stopped. Again, I froze, my arm reaching out from under the desk, my hand still on the bottom of the drawer. For a good thirty seconds I stayed like that. As still as a statue. My arm hurt and my hand was shaking.

Finally, the men resumed their conversation. With a silent sigh of relief, I dropped back into the cubby hole under the desk. I hadn't managed to close the drawer all the way. But at least it was no longer sticking out and noticeable from halfway across the room. Thick dull cigar smoke filled the air and turned my stomach. Cigarette smoke was bad enough. Why did men go in for such disgusting habits? Listening, I caught words here and there. I made a mental note of words like *Britanskiy*, Britain, and *Nemtsy*, Germans. I also made a mental note to study more languages when I got home—if I got home.

Wait. Had one of the men just said *Ambassador Plot*? In English? Could he be referring to Operation Ambassadors? I pricked up my ears and concentrated on the men's animated conversation. If only they'd switch to English, or French, or even German, I'd have a chance. The stranger had used a series of words I understood perfectly. Proper names. The names of the men involved in Operation Ambassadors. Iron Victor's companion had just rattled off: Robert Lockhart, Sidney Reilly, Boris Savinkov, Lieutenant Archibald Somersby, and Captain Clifford Douglas. Oh no. Not Archie! And Clifford. My hand flew to my mouth, and I stifled a gasp. Why Clifford? Wasn't he merely Kitty's chaperone? I had to warn them.

"Ambassador Plot." I was right. My ears hadn't deceived me. The stranger repeated those two words in English. Followed by names again. "*Dvoynoy agent.*" Then something else I couldn't make out in Russian. Then "Lieutenant Archibald Somersby." I didn't understand everything. But I had understood *Ambassador Plot* and *double agent* and Archibald Somersby. Archie? My heart sank. Was Archie a double agent? Fredricks had always insisted Archie was a double agent. Or was Archie a special target? Whichever, this was bad news. Very bad news. The head of the Cheka secret police knew about Operation Ambassadors. I felt like someone had socked me in the gut. I squeezed my eyes shut and wrapped my arms around my torso.

One of the agents involved in Operation Ambassadors was a mole, and the Cheka were setting a trap to catch the others.

Good heavens. If Iron Victor had an informant among the ambassadors, then he also must know I'd been sent to spy on him. A prickling sensation crept down my arms. I was in grave danger. Another reason to get out of here as soon as possible.

KITTY'S INTERLUDE
10 MARCH, 6 A.M.

A cold wind penetrated Kitty's wool coat and froze her eyelashes. Good thing she'd worn her fencing stockings under her skirt. She inhaled the frosty air. The rising sun kissed the domes of the Chudov Monastery and turned the frigid air a rosy pink. Kitty's favorite color. She stuffed her hands in her coat pockets and pulled the coat closer. Her fingers brushed against one of the dog treats she always carried with her. Too bad Poppy had to stay back at the consulate with Uncle Clifford. She smiled to herself. Clifford spoiled the pup something terrible. The little furball was probably enjoying a breakfast of fresh cream and blini pancakes. The pup wouldn't miss these dry old dog biscuits. Kitty threw them to a stray dog shivering in a doorway.

Glancing at her watch, Kitty took up her position outside the Kremlin Senate. Six in the morning, on the dot. Her job was to act as lookout and provide a distraction if necessary. Distractions were her forte, especially when she wore blonde ringlets and lowcut pink frills. Men couldn't resist a vampy baby doll. The saps. The lorry pulled up out front as planned. *Markov Gruzchiki,* Markov Removals, was painted across the side of the vehicle.

Wearing denims, work boots, and fake mustaches, Robert Lockhart and Sidney Reilly stepped out of the lorry. With their newsboy caps pulled low over their foreheads, they approached the guards. Lockhart pulled papers from the side pocket of his jacket and presented them. Per the plan, he explained that Comrade Lenin wanted everything set up before he arrived later this morning. The guard examined the papers and then waved them through. Stage one of Operation Ambassadors was a go.

The Russian, Boris Savinkov, leaned against the lorry smoking a cigarette. He was hardly recognizable in his denim work clothes. When Lockhart and Reilly returned from reconnoitering, the three men carried furniture from the back of the lorry into the Kremlin. Back and forth they went, lugging heavy desks, crystal lamps, upholstered chairs, and one very large trunk that took all of them to convey it inside. Wouldn't Comrades Lenin and Trotsky be surprised when they opened it.

After Lockhart and the other men had unloaded the furniture, they climbed back into the lorry and drove off. Stage one of Operation Ambassadors was complete. Now, on to stage two. At least Kitty would be inside for this part of the plan. She rubbed her hands together and headed toward the guards.

9

AN ALL-NIGHTER

How long had I been trapped under this desk? I wiggled my toes in my shoes to see if they were still there. I had to get out of this confounded library and warn my friends. But how? I couldn't just pop out from under the desk and waltz across the room in front of Iron Victor and his comrade. Still, Kitty and Clifford, not to mention Archie, were in imminent danger. I had to think of something. A mole in Operation Ambassadors could mean death by firing squad. The Cheka police would come down hard on would-be assassins. And imagine the international scandal if it came out that Allied diplomats had tried to kill Soviet leaders to keep Russia fighting against the Germans.

The man visiting Iron Victor. Was he one of the ambassadors? The mole? I pricked up my ears and listened to see if I recognized his voice. He was speaking Russian, of course. But all the ambassadors spoke Russian—Lockhart, Reilly, Savinkov, the whole lot of them. For all I knew, Archie spoke Russian, too. No. I would recognize Archie's voice, even in Russian. And it definitely wasn't Clifford. I'd know his voice anywhere. If only I could get a look at him. Did I dare creep out from under the desk and take a peek?

My long limbs were an impediment to maneuvering in such a confined space. There wasn't enough room for me to twist onto my hands and knees without risking raising a ruckus. Curses. I wished Iron Victor and his guest would finish and leave the library so I could make my escape. I had to report to the consulate. Operation Ambassadors was a setup. If I was right and there was a mole in the operation, then the Cheka knew everything.

Who was the mole? Young Lockhart? He seemed a good enough chap. That slick Sidney Reilly? By the looks of him, he could talk the stripes off a Siberian tiger. But looks can be deceiving. Just look at me, expert file clerk become international spy. The Russian Savinkov might fit the bill. The factions and crossings and double-crossings in Russian politics was beyond my paygrade or my clearance level. That left only Archie. I forced my mind to close the lid on that idea.

Fingering the envelope, I turned my thoughts back to the White Rose Directive. My gut told me that the royal family was in danger. Poor Natasha, worried about her husband. Were the rumors true? Had Michael escaped? Was he leading a counter-revolution? And what was Fredricks's role in all this? He knew the Russians would sign the peace treaty on 3 March. He knew they'd move the capital from Petrograd to Moscow on 10 March. And he knew about the White Rose Directive. Apparently, he was posing as a Russian duke, Duke Zakrevsky. And, as usual, he had his finger in every important pie.

Shuffling sounds signaled that the men were on the move. Their voices were coming in this direction. Speaking of firing squads. I held my knees tight to my chest and grimaced. Squeezing my eyes shut, I listened. One of the men pounded on the desk. I sucked in air and then held my breath. Their voices were raised in a heated disagreement. A clunk on the desk top. I surmised that one of the men had dropped something on the desk. Another envelope? A file folder? More secret documents? An ultimatum?

I cringed. What would happen when Iron Victor noticed the top drawer was cracked open? He would realize someone had broken into his desk. I pulled my feet even closer to my bottom. I could feel the presence of the men on the other side of the desk panel. In fact, the toe of a black boot poked under the back of the desk. I felt like swatting at it. Go away! Strong cologne wafted under the desk. The smell of grapefruit. I tried to remember the scent Iron Victor wore. Was it his cologne or his comrade's? Could I identify the man by his smell? If it was Archie or Fredricks, I could. Archie smelled like citrus and pine, and Fredricks smelled like sandalwood and sin.

Good heavens. My name. One of the men said "Fiona Figg." Or was I hallucinating? I had been under this blooming desk all night. Why were they talking about me? What? Now they were talking about Maria Bochkareva, aka Happy. Could the file folder be information from prison? Were the police looking for us? We had escaped prison. It did stand to reason. I hoped to heaven the file didn't include pictures. Otherwise, my goose was cooked.

The voices receded again. Thank goodness. By some miracle, Iron Victor didn't notice his desk drawer was unlocked. Or, if he did, he didn't react. Maybe he didn't want to say anything in front of his guest. I exhaled. *Please leave now. Please. Please. Please.* I really needed to stretch and get out from under this desk. More importantly, I had to warn my friends.

My eyelids were heavy and I was nodding off. The lack of sleep was catching up with me, too. *Ouch!* I grabbed my calf. What a time to get a cramp. Being tall helped me pass as a man in disguise, but it was deuced inconvenient when hiding under a desk.

Hugging myself, I distracted myself from the pain by concentrating on what the men were saying. If I delivered a helpful report to Captain Hall and the War Office, then my sins might be forgiven, and all would be well. Back to how it was before I flew the coop, back when I was an award-winning British operative and not a love-struck sap falling for an enemy spy.

The men were still going at it. Arguing. At least they were back on the other side of the room. I listened for key phrases such as Ambassador Plot and White Rose Directive. Even in Russian, I'd recognize those. Instead, the men seemed to be arguing about the use of violence to quell counter-revolution. Iron Victor was in favor. His comrade, not so much.

There was a soft rap on the library door. Did Iron Victor always conduct his business in the middle of the night? The butler announced a visitor. Duke Pavel Zakrevsky. My hand flew to my mouth to stifle a gasp.

Duke Zakrevsky. Fredricks! What in heaven's name was he doing here?

He was back from the Bug. Did he know I was here? In Moscow? That I'd accepted his invitation, was put in jail, and had gone undercover as Iron Victor's governess? Somehow, the rotter always knew where I was and what I was doing.

Rustling sounds signaled movement in the room as the men greeted the duke. Iron Victor's jovial tone suggested he was a fan. Even speaking Russian, I recognized Fredricks's smooth baritone. Was I imagining things, or did I catch a whiff of sandalwood? I closed my eyes and inhaled. Big mistake. Memories of our recent time together in London came flooding back. Seeing Fredricks standing on my threshold dripping blood from a bullet wound.

Hiding him in my flat and nursing him back to health. His graceful beauty as he slept on my sofa. His lips on mine... *Get a grip, Fiona. Now is not the time to indulge romantic fantasies.*

When the butler announced another visitor, I snapped out of my reminiscence. Countess Natalia Romanov. She purred Victor's name and I could imagine her imperious waltz into the room with graceful arms cutting the air. So, she did escape. And she'd found Fredricks, aka the duke, and persuaded him to plead her case to Iron Victor. Did Duke Zakrevsky have that kind of influence? It shouldn't surprise me if he did.

From what I could make out, Fredricks was reporting on the peace talk in Brest-Litovsk, boasting about his role in the negotiations. Iron Victor agreed now they weren't fighting foreign enemies, they could turn their attention to the country's domestic enemies—tsarists, counter-revolutionaries, and Cossacks. Fredricks seemed to take issue with Iron Victor's stance on the Cossacks, arguing that no minority group should be persecuted for its ethnic identity.

If I understood him correctly, he'd recounted the story of a friend's parents who had been killed by the British army when, just a boy, his friend had hidden in a closet. I'd heard Fredricks tell that story many times. It was the story not of a friend, but rather his own story. His family was executed by the British army right in front of his eyes. Imagine a boy seeing such a thing. No wonder he hated the British. I shook my head and pushed the horrific thoughts from my mind.

"Do you smell peaches?" Fredricks asked in English.

Peaches? My cheeks warmed. For some unfathomable reason, Fredricks always said I smelled like peaches. The rogue couldn't know I was here, could he? I squeezed my eyes shut and waited for him to sniff me out. He was an expert tracker.

Thankfully, the countess seized the opportunity to change the subject. At first, her tone was polite, even deferential, but as she concluded her impassioned speech, she became haughty and demanding. I thought of my grandmother's favorite saying: You catch more flies with honey than with vinegar.

Iron Victor responded that the royal family posed a threat to the Bolshevik government and, until they were contained, the Soviet state would be unstable. I was pretty sure that's what he'd said, although memorizing the dictionary only took me so far in understanding the language. As my grandmother would say, "Many a slip between cup and lip."

"Why not send Michael and his brother Nicholas to the Brits? England deserves the tyrant." Fredricks spoke in favor of shipping the entire royal family off to England. "Nicholas and George are cousins, after all."

"The British royal family won't have them." Iron Victor switched to English. "The Romanovs are poison. They've infected Russia. And even his cousin knows better than to take that risk in England."

"King George fears bringing the Romanovs to England will spread anti-monarchist sentiments," the other male visitor said, also in English. "Then it will be his neck on the line."

"The English monarchy are a despicable lot." Iron Victor chuckled. "But they're not stupid."

"Not all English are despicable," Fredricks said. "There is one particular lady I quite adore." My skin prickled. *He knows I'm here.* The cad. Why wasn't he giving me away?

"And what about Michael?" the countess demanded. "Surely he cannot be held accountable for the sins of his brother."

"Your husband is not the threat," Iron Victor said. "The threat is what he represents. To Russia he represents the past. To England he represents the future. And to both, he's undesirable."

"People should be judged for who they are and not what they represent." The countess spat out the words.

Iron Victor said something I couldn't translate, and the men laughed. The countess had been silenced. From across the room, I could feel her sulking. I sympathized. It was far too easy for men to dismiss the words of a woman because they never expect women to act on those words. Someday, men's underestimation of women will return to bite them in the bottom.

The tone of the men's conversation became lighter. I hoped that meant they were wrapping up, and I could finally get out from under this cramped desk. I was encouraged when Fredricks bid them farewell, taking the countess with him. I heard her heels clicking on the tiles as she left the room. Unfortunately, it seemed the other man had stayed on. Drat. Would I ever get out from under this blooming desk?

Iron Victor (presumably it was him) put on the phonograph, Stravinsky's "The Fox" again. Instead of preparing to call it a night, they were settling in. To make matters worse, I could no longer hear a word they were saying. Relaxing into the corner under the desk, I resigned myself to continued confinement. Even the adrenaline coursing through my veins couldn't compete with too many sleepless nights in jail and then that horrible prison hospital. Still holding the purloined envelope on my lap, I stretched my legs as far as I could and leaned back against the desk.

I may or may not have dozed off a few times. *Can you blame me?* I'd been hiding under the desk for hours. My calves were still cramping, and I desperately needed sleep. More than anything, I needed to escape and warn Kitty and Clifford that there was a mole among the ambassadors. Hopefully it wasn't Archie. No. Archie couldn't be working for the Germans. He was a patriot. I pushed the thought away and let my mind wander back to my grandparents' farm. I closed my eyes and drifted back to those lazy afternoons hiding in the barn reading stories. The smell of the hay. The warmth of the sun coming through the open rafters. The roughness of the bales against my legs.

I rubbed my eyes. Good grief. How long had I been asleep?

If my watch was right, Iron Victor and his visitor had been at it all night. The way they'd been shouting and carrying on earlier, it was a wonder the whole household didn't wake up. I listened for the men's voices. They sounded different. Perhaps lack of sleep was affecting them too. One of them was delivering a monologue about socialism spreading in Europe. The passion in his voice made me shudder.

"The fatherland is in danger." Heavens. "Defend the fatherland." Did he need to shout?

He stopped. I pricked up my ears. A clicking sound and then nothing. No voices. No movement. Utter stillness. Had the men left the library? If so, they were as quiet as mice. What were they doing out there? I rolled onto hands and knees and crawled out from under the desk. My whole body was stiff from spending hours contorted into a cube. I listened again. Nothing. Kneeling, I peeked up over the desk. The chairs and sofa were empty. The men had left. Finally. Thank goodness.

I slid the desk drawer open and replaced the envelope. My legs wobbled. Gripping the edge of the desk for stability, I managed to stand up. I gave each of my legs a good shake. Slowly, I emerged from behind the desk. My heart raced as I tiptoed out into the open. Glancing around, I confirmed the room was empty. I approached the sitting area, where the men had been just minutes before. My hand flew to my mouth, and I stifled a scream.

His head cocked back at an unnatural angle, his lifeless eyes staring up at the ceiling, his limbs rigid, Iron Victor's body was sprawled out on the floor between the coffee table and his high-backed chair.

Iron Victor was dead.

Kitty giggled and flirted with the guards. Posing as one of the cleaning staff, she produced a small feather duster from her coat pocket and used it to caress the cheek of the most recalcitrant guard. She made sure the top buttons of her coat were open and her lowcut maid's outfit was visible. With its frills and feathers, it was more tarty fancy-dress costume than actual maid's outfit. The better to get what she wanted. Which, at this moment, was to gain access to the Kremlin State Building and the office of Comrade Vladimir Lenin. British Intelligence reported that Lenin and his commissar Leon Trotsky were meeting in just under two hours to make final arrangements for their move from Petrograd.

Her decolletage worked like a charm and within ten minutes, she was standing in the center of Lenin's new office suite.

Kitty took advantage of the empty suite to have a look around. In the middle of a narrow room stood a very long table covered in a green cloth. Obviously the conference room. There were a good twenty armless chairs on either side of the table. In the corner was a small desk upon which sat a typewriting machine. Attached to one wall was a wooden case that held several maps that could be unrolled from their spools. Beyond the conference room was the office.

Lenin's office was decorated in deep scarlet, carpets, drapes, upholstery, all red—appropriate for their government-sanctioned bloodbath. A half-full bookcase with glass doors stood behind a large wooden desk. Next to the desk were several boxes. Probably more books. Kitty didn't trust people who spent too much time with their noses in books. Like Aunt Fiona and her ridiculous Sherlock Holmes stories. Why read about life when you can step outside your door and live it?

She pulled the feather duster from her coat pocket and pretended to dust. She was a trained operative and nothing escaped her attention. Not even a speck of dust. She glanced at her watch. One hour until show time.

She spotted it across the room. On the far wall there were three telephone boxes. Under the telephones sat the trunk the men had delivered earlier. Kitty went to the trunk and knocked twice. The trunk knocked back. She smiled. The plan was set.

10

LOOKING FOR CLUES

Kneeling next to Iron Victor's body, I quickly felt his neck for a pulse. Shivers ran up my spine. He was cold as ice and his lips were a sickly blue. What in heaven's name had happened? Judging from his body temperature, he'd been dead for some time. And yet I'd heard someone speaking to him just a few minutes ago. I glanced at my watch. Not yet seven. Soon the maid would arrive with coffee or Mrs. V would come looking for her husband. Not a minute to lose. I set to work.

Still on my knees, I surveyed the room for clues as to what had happened. There was no blood. I didn't see any knife wounds or bullet holes. Iron Victor's body was intact. Had he just keeled over from a heart attack? Or perhaps a stroke? He'd looked like a healthy man in his forties. All extremely suspicious. Minutes earlier he'd been in a nocturnal meeting with two comrades, one of them Fredrick Fredricks, and now he was dead.

Frantically, I scanned the scene. Before the maid or his wife appeared, I had to ascertain how Iron Victor died. Quickly, I made a mental list to guide my search. First, I had to determine whether he'd been murdered or died of natural causes. If it was murder, then I had to establish the means and find the murder weapon. Then there were the suspects. I surveyed the room. Was there any way for a killer to get in unnoticed? There was only one entrance and exit. The main door to the hallway. If Victor was murdered, the killer came through that door. And he—or she—did so while I was under that bloody desk.

Except for the dead body lying on the floor, nothing in the room had been disturbed. Everything was exactly as it had been when I'd had my interview a few days ago—the high-backed chair, the phonograph cabinet, the sofa and matching chairs around the fireplace. None of the bookcases had been troubled. At least not that I could tell. Then again, there were so many books, if one or two were missing, I'd never know. Surely the man couldn't have been killed for a couple of books.

Since no one could have snuck in unnoticed through a window or back entrance, if it was foul play, his nocturnal visitors were the most likely suspects: the countess, the mystery man, and Fredricks. I sat back on my haunches and ran through their possible motives.

The mystery man told Iron Victor about the Ambassador Plot. Why would he do that and then kill him? And why wait until the wee hours of the morning when he could have killed him earlier? It didn't make sense. The mystery man and Victor had been carrying on all night like conspirators. Had I missed something? A betrayal, perhaps? And if not the mystery man, then who?

The countess hated Iron Victor and the Cheka for imprisoning her husband. Would she go so far as murder to get revenge? He'd all but laughed in her face. She had motive. She had opportunity. Except when she and Fredricks left, Victor was still alive. And she couldn't very well have murdered him in front of an audience. Maybe she slipped something into his drink. That could account for the lack of blood or wounds and the delay between her leaving and his death. I made a mental note to put the countess at the top of my list of suspects.

And then there was Fredricks. A suspected assassin of double agents, Fredricks was always on my list. But why would Fredricks kill the head of the Russian secret police? My head was spinning. It didn't make any sense. If Fredricks had killed Iron Victor, then what? The third man had stayed to watch him die and then delivered a speech over the dead body? How had Fredricks done it? Something bloodless. His preferred method of killing. Poison. Which would also explain why I didn't hear a struggle.

If only Kitty were here, she could dust for fingerprints and test for poison. There had to be some evidence as to what happened. Four empty glasses sat on the low coffee table. Removing my handkerchief from a shirt pocket, gingerly I picked up the glass closest to Iron Victor. Examining the few remaining drops of amber liquid, I sniffed. The smell of whiskey and something else... but what? Something floral. Not rose. Not carnation. I sniffed the glass again. Floral and spicy. The lingering scent of jasmine. Cringing, I leaned closer to the dead man's face and sniffed. If he'd been poisoned, then perhaps I could smell the poison on him. Some poisons like cyanide left a distinctive almond smell. Was there a poison that smelled like jasmine? Did Russians drink jasmine-scented whiskey? Was the countess wearing jasmine perfume? Where in the blazes did the smell originate?

Carefully, I lifted the lapel of the dead man's suitcoat. Intact and clean, his white shirt showed no sign of blood or a wound. I gritted my teeth and reached into the interior jacket pocket. My fingers brushed against a hard case. I withdrew it. A leather cigar case. I pulled off the top to reveal two empty slots and one occupied by a thin cigar. I slid the cigarillo out of its case. It had a band decorated with a woman's face. She had a red flower in her long black hair. The label read, "La Aroma de Cuba." I smelled it. Earthy and spicy. Much better unlit than producing foul smoke. I slid the cigar back into its case and replaced the case in Victor's pocket.

My legs began to cramp again. I could kneel no longer. Unless I wanted to be stuck squatting next to a corpse, I simply had to get to my feet. Perhaps another perspective on the scene would be useful.

In the center of the coffee table, a glass ashtray overflowed with cigarette butts, the tail ends of several cigarillos, and two thin cigars, one of them only partially smoked. The cigar label featured an image of a clown that I recognized at once as Punch, the popular comedic figure. The two dark cigars were outliers in the filthy bunch. I glanced around to make sure no one was coming and then plucked the cigar butts out of the dish, rolled them in a handkerchief, and dropped them into my skirt pocket. Disgusting, but necessary. Anyway, I couldn't very well dump the whole bloody ashtray into my pocket.

I glanced at my watch again. Just after seven. How much longer did I have to investigate? I'd learned from Sherlock Holmes stories that no detail is too small. Anything could be significant. And I'd learned the principle of exchange from Kitty's studies in forensics. Whenever two people or objects come in contact, there will be an exchange of material. No matter how miniscule, the killer always leaves something and takes something from the scene of the crime. What the killer carries away: traces of the victim's skin under a fingernail; a hair transported from the head of the victim on a coat. Or what the killer leaves behind: fingerprints; lipstick; muddy boot prints. The best way to prove guilt was to match the two, what the killer took and what the killer left.

I zipped around the circumference of the room. What had I

missed? Was anything different now from yesterday? The phonograph stood open. Yes. Iron Victor had been playing Stravinsky's "The Fox." I continued around the room, looking up and down the bookcases. Nothing out of place. Except for the corpse, the sitting area was exactly as it had been. Two upholstered chairs, the matching sofa, and one high-backed throne around a low table. Apart from the file folder on the desk, nothing else had been moved. The stained-glass lamp, the gold inkwell and pen set sat exactly where they'd been before.

On my way past the fireplace, I looked up at the Kandinsky painting. Wait. Something was off. I strode over to take a closer look. My word. The painting was ajar. One corner had peeled away from the fireplace hood. I leaned in and peeked behind the frame. Golly. One side of the frame was attached to two hinges so that the painting opened like a door. Using just a fingernail, I pushed it open. Inside the wooden hood was a secret compartment nestled behind the painting. Could this be what the killer was after? Something in this compartment. I glanced around and then used the tips of my fingers to pry open the compartment door.

The wall safe contained jewelry boxes, a stack of notes, and a gun. I opened one of the jewelry boxes to find a gorgeous pearl necklace. Another held the biggest diamond I'd ever seen set in a necklace adorned with rubies. Could it be real? And that stack of cash. Golly. If this was a robbery, it had gone wrong. What thief would leave priceless jewelry and that much money? If the killer had taken something, I had no idea what.

A commotion from the entryway startled me. I stepped away from the fireplace. Shouting, Mrs. V rushed at me. When she saw her husband sprawled out on the floor, she stopped. The blood drained from her face, and she let out a silent scream.

"I can explain." I approached her. Of course, I couldn't

explain. I couldn't explain anything. I had no idea what had happened to her husband or why.

With murder in her eyes, she came at me and shoved me so hard that I fell back into the high-backed chair.

Good heavens. She must think that *I* killed him!

KITTY'S INTERLUDE
10 MARCH, 8 A.M.

Pretending to dust, Kitty examined every item in the Kremlin office. True, her training in forensics had given her an eye for details. Still, she didn't have Aunt Fiona's photographic memory. Speaking of... How was Fiona getting along in the nursery, wiping bums? She smiled. The way Aunt Fiona pined for children, she was probably in her element playing pass the slipper and wiping drool off chins. A dog was enough responsibility for Kitty. She needed to be free to travel and explore the world. She'd go mad cooped up in a nursery with snot-nosed brats all day.

Kitty glanced at her watch. Nearly eight. Lenin and Trotsky were due any minute. And so were the men from the telephone company. Since they had three telephones, they needed three men. At least that was the plan. She had the plan down pat. In her mind, she rehearsed it again anyway.

As soon as Lenin and Trotsky arrived, she was to signal to the men from the hall window. Her job was to keep watch while, disguised as men from the telephone company there to connect the phones, the ambassadors stormed the office and captured the heads of the Bolshevik government. Archie had their guns hidden

in the trunk with him. When he heard Lockhart use the word
"*zvonit*" or "ring," that was Archie's cue to jump out of the trunk,
toss guns to the other men, and kidnap Lenin and Trotsky. Then
the men would bind and gag the Bolsheviks, stuff them in the
trunk, and transport them out of the building.

Easy-peasy.

FLEEING THE SCENE

I tried to calm Mrs. V, but it was no use. She was hysterical. She kept pointing at me and shrieking. I had to make my escape. Otherwise, with all her racket, no doubt the library soon would be overrun with the staff. In a matter of seconds, Mrs. V's face went from bright red to sheet white. With one last screech, she collapsed in a heap on the floor. She'd fainted.

I fought the instinct to revive her. It was only a matter of time before the staff arrived and called the police to cart me off. I had to get out of this house and warn my friends about Operation Ambassadors. It wasn't safe. There was a mole among them. More to the point, I couldn't let the Cheka take me. Not again. I couldn't spend another night in a Bolshevik jail. My sanity wouldn't survive.

With new resolve to save my own skin, I scanned the scene one last time. Could I snag Iron Victor's whiskey glass? A bulging glass would be noticeable in my pocket. Anyway, I didn't know which was his. And I certainly couldn't cart off all four glasses. If the killer poisoned the whiskey, surely, he—or she—wouldn't drink from it. But if the whiskey was poisoned then all four drinkers should have died, or at least be feeling the effects. Were the others in hospital or sick? Possible, but not probable. Unless, of course, the perpetrator intended to kill the entire party. Sure, Iron Victor might have died of natural causes after his guests left. But given the political intrigue in Moscow, I suspected foul play. Unfortunately, so did Mrs. V, who seemed convinced I was the culprit. I stared down at her. Still out like a light. Thank goodness. I had to make my escape.

A murmuring from the doorway caught my attention. Drat. The children. They stood quarreling at the threshold. I couldn't let them see their father dead and their mother unconscious. What would they think? They'd be scarred for life. No, they didn't need to see the grisly scene. I hurried to intercept them and herd them back to the nursery. It was the least I could do for dear little Anna. I'd grown quite fond of her.

Taking the boys' hands and nattering on to Anna about the *Wizard of Oz*, I shepherded the children upstairs to the nursery. The boys were full of questions about what had happened in the library. I deflected as best as I could. Poor little mites had just lost their father. He may have been Iron Victor to others, but he was Papa to them.

"Why were you in the library?" Vitya asked.

"Father had meetings all night," Anna said with a knowing tone. "They came and went."

I stopped in the middle of the staircase and turned to her. "Did you see them?"

She nodded. "I was sleepwalking."

Sleepwalking my eye. Spying more like. "Can you describe them, the people you saw? Had you seen them before?"

She rolled her eyes at me and huffed.

"Tell me what you saw." Judging by her face, my tone was a

tad too rough. "Please, dear. Might you please tell me what you saw?"

"A man I'd seen before." She started up the stairs again.

"Go on," I said encouragingly.

"Tall with long black hair and funny clothes." She giggled. "His trousers puffed out and then disappeared into big black boots." She demonstrated. "And he had a long stick with little leather strips on the end." She flicked her wrist and pretended to swat a pony.

Fredricks. His jodhpurs and riding stick. So, he'd been here before. "Does the man come to visit your father often?"

"Sometimes." She nodded. "He's very important."

"Why do you say that?"

"The way Papa acts." Anna stopped and looked thoughtful. She put her finger to her front tooth. "When the man visits, Papa brings out the special whiskey in the crystal bottle."

Interesting. "Anyone else visit last night?"

She scrunched up her nose. "A bear."

"A bear?" I was beginning to think she really was sleep-walking.

"Black hair that went all the way around his face and head." She made a circle around her face.

I squinted at her. "You mean a beard?"

She nodded.

"Had he been here before?"

"No." She shook her head.

"Are you sure?" I leaned down to look her in the eyes.

"I sleepwalk every night to watch who visits Papa." Her lip trembled and she seemed younger. She was old enough to know something wasn't right.

"It's okay." I held her gaze. "It's our secret." Too bad I couldn't take the child with me. I'd love to find out everything she knew about her father's late-night meetings. "Did you see anyone else last night?"

"A pretty lady." Anna nodded. "She was with the funny big man."

The countess and Fredricks. That tracked with what I'd heard. And the bear must be our mystery man.

"And one more." She held up her index finger.

"A fifth person?" I'd heard only Iron Victor, the countess, Fredricks, and the mystery man. Was there another person? Someone I didn't hear come in?

"A man with the face of a lady." She scrunched up her face.

I didn't know whether to believe her. A bear. A man with a lady's face. "Why do you say he looked like a lady?" I had been known to dress as a man. Perhaps it was someone in disguise.

She caressed her cheek. "Smooth face and pretty eyes with long eyelashes like a lady." Maybe it really was a woman. A woman dressed like a man. Had this man-lady snuck in and murdered Iron Victor?

"What else did you notice about her, er, him?" I put my hand on her shoulder.

"He smelled good." She smiled.

She must have gotten close to the killer. "What did he smell like?"

"Mama's perfume."

A man with a face of a lady who smelled like her mother's perfume. I was starting to think she was an unreliable witness. Unfortunately, I didn't have more time to question her. I had to install the children in the nursery and then take my leave. "Anything else you remember about the bear?"

"His eyebrows looked like caterpillars." She stroked her own brows.

Beard and bushy eyebrows. Not Archie then. Unless he was in

disguise. Both the Russian revolutionary and Sidney Reilly could fit that description, especially if they added a bit more facial hair. The man-lady. That one baffled me. Unless Fredricks left and came back dressed as a woman. He'd been known to don a disguise now and then, too.

"And there was a fairy with pink hair and green skin." She held out a strand of her own hair. "And a flying monkey."

"A fairy?" Now I knew she was imagining things. I may not know who killed Iron Victor, but I knew it was not a green-skinned fairy or a flying monkey. "Come on, children."

After I hustled the children into the nursery, I went through to my room and gathered up my belongs, such as they were. While stuffing my smalls into my valise, I formulated my next move. I would take a taxi to the consulate. Hopefully I could get a taxi. And hopefully I could get there in time to stop Operation Ambassadors before my colleagues were trapped by the Cheka. I wished I'd heard more of their plans. What day were they going to the Kremlin Senate to kidnap or assassinate Misters Lenin and Trotsky?

Dashing out of the nursery, my suitcase in hand, I ran down the stairs. As I crossed the foyer, I nearly slammed into a kitchen maid. She gave me a strange look but didn't stop. Neither did I. By now, the rest of the staff would be in the library gnashing their teeth over their dead master and fainting mistress. Making my escape, I hurried across the foyer and out the front door.

The air was nipping. I wrapped my coat tighter. In my hurry, I'd forgotten my hat. Bother. I wasn't going back for it. Better to lose my hat than my head. At least this time, I'd made my escape fully clothed and wearing shoes.

Lightly falling snow dotted my face. I looked up and down the street. Where could I catch a taxicab? I should have paid more attention when Kitty brought me here. Where exactly was here?

Wind to my back, I headed for the corner. Blown along, I was halfway there when a shiny black car passed me. I turned and watched it pull up in front of Iron Victor's house. Three men in suits jumped out and strode to the front door. The Cheka. Resisting the urge to gawk, I turned back and quickened my pace.

A bus pulled up to the corner and I hopped on. I had no idea where I was going but I knew enough to get away from the scene of the crime. Mrs. V would surely have me arrested. The further the bus went, the larger the gardens got. We were heading out of the city. I wished I was on a bus to my flat in Northwick Terrace. I'd had enough of Moscow. And yet I had to get off this blooming bus and get back to the consulate and warn my friends.

By the time I had circumnavigated the city on a series of buses and found my way back to the consulate, I was completely knackered. Not to mention freezing. Hopefully, the ambassadors were there and hadn't left yet to carry out their plan to kidnap Vladimir Lenin. A plan that sounded downright barmy to me. Why would the British government risk an international scandal? Ah, right. To get Russia back into the war. Were they really so important to the war effort? From what Happy had said, the Russian army was a shambles and full of deserters and mutineers. She had claimed the Women's Battalion of Death was all that was left of the Russian defenses against the Germans... and the Bolsheviks. I didn't doubt the Women's Battalion of Death could hold their own. Where was Happy now? And Natasha? Was she still with Fredricks? No time for questions. I must warn the ambassadors.

My feet dragging, I climbed the stairs to the consulate. I dreaded telling Kitty what had happened. I'd failed in my assignment. And now I couldn't go back to Iron Victor's house. I'd be lucky if the police didn't find me and cart me off to jail. Mrs. V had found me standing over the body of her dead husband. If I didn't ascertain the true killer, I would be spending the rest of my life in a Russian prison. I hoped to heaven Kitty could find some clue on the cigar butts tucked away in my pocket. Otherwise, I didn't have much to go on besides the scent of jasmine—except of course Anna's furry bear, man-lady, and pink-haired fairy.

As soon as I knocked on the door, the barking began. Poppy was small but fierce. Clifford opened the door. "I say, aren't you supposed to be watching some nippers or some such?" He clamped his pipe between his teeth.

I pushed past him. "Where is everyone?" Poppy trotted behind me as I dashed from the main room to the lavatory and back again. "Where have they gone?" Please tell me they haven't already put Operation Ambassadors into motion. Heaven help them. "It's a trap." My pulse quickened. "We have to find them." I stopped at the table and stared down at the map of Moscow.

"What's all this about a trap?" Clifford sauntered over to me. "Calm down, old thing." He put his hand on my arm. "You're going to blow a gasket," he said, his blue eyes filled with concern.

"Kitty, Archie..." I put a hand to either side of my face. "They're in grave danger."

"What are you on about?" Clifford took my elbow and led me to a chair. "Sit down and I'll fetch you a drink." His answer to every crisis was a strong drink. "And then you can tell me what's going on." He went to a side table and poured out two brandies.

"There's a mole. One of the ambassadors. The Cheka know about the plan. It's a trap." My mind was racing. "We have to stop them. They'll be caught." Breathless, I tried to remember the exact plans. "How long ago did they leave?"

Clifford handed me a brandy. "Drink up, old girl." Glass in hand, he sat down in a chair next to me. "Then tell me what the devil is going on."

I told him about the library and Iron Victor's nocturnal visitors and what I'd heard. How the mystery man had named each one of the ambassadors. How he'd singled out Archie. "I'm telling you they know."

"Someone told them." Clifford's countenance clouded over. "Good lord. Kitty. She's with them." He jumped up and Poppy barked. Clifford scooped her up. "We've got to warn them."

Finally. "That's what I've been saying." I stood up and tugged on the bottom of my jacket. "Where are they?"

Clifford looked at his watch. "They're inside the Kremlin Senate by now." He put Poppy back on the floor. "What should we do?" He ran a comb through his thinning hair. "Our Kitty is in danger."

I threw my hands in the air. "That's what I've been trying to tell you!" I flew into action. I grabbed Poppy's leash and attached it to her collar. She was a good little bloodhound. "What are you waiting for?" On my way out, I grabbed a hat from a hook near the door—one of Kitty's little woolen sailor numbers.

Clifford fetched his coat and hat from the coat rack.

"Come on." I wrapped the end of Poppy's leash around my hand. "Let's go."

KITTY'S INTERLUDE
10 MARCH, 8.30 A.M.

Kitty paced the office. The Bolsheviks were late. They were supposed to be at the Kremlin half an hour ago. The ambassadors would be freezing their arses off waiting outside for her signal. She dusted the typewriter for the tenth time. Where were they? She wanted to get this mission over and get back to Poppy. Crazy how much she missed the pup. Usually, she took Poppy along. But a housekeeper with a dog would be a dead giveaway. Especially today. Security was extra tight. No one was supposed to know the Bolshevik leaders arrived today. They'd told the newspapers that they would arrive tomorrow. But British intel was good. Best in the world.

She dropped into the desk chair and fiddled with the ink blotter. Come on, dammit. There was nothing she hated more than waiting.

"How are you doing in there? Still alive?" She bent over the trunk.

Archie's muffled voice answered. "Barely."

Footfalls and then a jingling sound outside the door made her jump. She adjusted her maid's outfit, smoothed a loose hair back into her chignon, and readied her feather duster. The moment of truth. Duster in hand, she stood at attention, listening. Men's voices. She darted to the window and ran the duster over the windowsill. As soon as the door to the office opened, she gave the signal. A quick wave of the duster and then back to wiping the sill.

Two men entered the room. She recognized them immediately as the Bolshevik leaders. She'd seen plenty of photographs in newspapers and in intelligence briefings. Vladimir Lenin entered first, followed by Leon Trotsky.

Lenin wore an ushanka fur cap and a heavy wool overcoat. He had a well-groomed mustache and beard, both lightly streaked with silver. There was an asymmetry to his face that made one eye look kindly and the other extremely stern. His brows were uneven too. The left arched into an upside-down letter V, while the right cut a slash across his forehead. He removed his coat and hat, revealing an impressive bald head and a pressed three-piece suit.

Trotsky had enough hair for both of them—it must have stood five inches high. He wore a messier version of the same mustache and beard. His prominent nose, vivid eyes, and tiny wire-rimmed glasses gave him the look of a predatory bird, a hawk maybe. As if to display the contradictions of Bolshevism, he wore a flawless olive peasant jacket that looked like it had never been worn. Kitty chuckled to herself. Hypocrites.

Ignoring her, Lenin sat behind his desk and Trotsky leaned against it. They were deep in conversation. They didn't even have a look around. It was obvious it didn't matter where they made their headquarters. Whatever was happening with them happened inside their minds and their words. They didn't need tables and chairs. Their world was furnished with ideas and speeches.

Ears pricked, she continued fake dusting. The Bolsheviks were discussing a parade scheduled for April. Nothing top-secret, unfortunately. A knock at the door indicated the arrival of the telephone installation crew. Trotsky answered the door. Unbothered by the interruption, he ushered the telephone men into the office. Kitty and Robert Lockhart exchanged glances. Lockhart and Reilly positioned themselves near the telephone boxes. Savinkov had stayed with the lorry. The men began fussing with the boxes. Reilly tapped at one box with his cane. He shouldn't have brought that cane. What telephone worker carried a cane to work? How stupid. He would give them away.

There it was. Lockhart gave the signal. "*Zvonit.*" A rifle in each hand, Archie exploded out of the trunk. He tossed one to Lockhart. Before it reached its target, the door flew open and a half-dozen Cheka rushed in. Dropping the duster, Kitty swung around. Lenin and Trotsky had disappeared into a panel in the wall behind the desk. Bloody hell. A secret passage.

How was she going to get out of this mess? Someone had tipped them off. She looked from Lockhart to Reilly to Archie. And Savinkov waiting outside. The ambassadors. Had one of them snitched?

"Everyone, get out." Archie crouched down in the trunk and started firing on the Cheka. "Now!"

They turned on him, guns blazing. He flipped the lid to the trunk shut. It had taken three blokes to carry it because it was reinforced with steel. Bullets riddled the closed trunk. Kitty winced. Dammit. What a mess.

A couple of Cheka had Lockhart restrained. Lockhart produced a knife from a sheath under his jacket and thrust it at his captors. One of the Cheka called to a mate, who leveled his gun and shot Lockhart in the leg. His mate helped him drag Lockhart from the room, blood trailing them out. After a couple of swipes with his cane, Reilly slipped behind the police and escaped through a window.

That left two more Cheka, and the two who were still firing on the trunk. Ignoring her. Just a stupid maid.

Kitty glided along the windows until she was behind them. She took a deep breath and then lunged forward. With a butterfly kick to the heads, she took out one and then another. The Cheka weren't ignoring her now. They both came at her. Another butterfly kick hit one on the jaw and the other in the neck, disarming them. Their rifles went flying. Kitty dove at one of the rifles. She grabbed it and rolled, firing on the Cheka as she went. Both men dropped.

Loud shouts from the hallway warned of more police. Grimacing, she took one last look at the trunk. Agents knew what they were getting into when they signed up. She had been trained not to sacrifice herself for a lost cause. Nothing else to be done. She took out the last two Cheka and then dropped the rifle. Smoothing her hair and maid's uniform, she exited the office, smiling at the police on her way past.

Dammit, Archie. She had to do something to buy him some time. With a loud screech, she feigned fainting and fell to the floor—making sure her coat fell open and the front of her dress came unbuttoned.

To a man, all half-dozen policemen ran to her side. One of them knelt and lifted her head. The others peered down at her exposed bosom.

She smiled and said in perfect Russian, "Oh, how silly of me. I must have taken a turn."

12

CRISIS AT THE KREMLIN

Clifford and I stood on the corner trying to hail a taxicab for ages. *Come on. Our friends are in danger.* I shifted from foot to foot. My eyes watered from the cold and my fingertips felt like icicles. Finally. A car stopped for us. When Clifford asked for the Kremlin Senate, the driver gave us a strange look. The car pulled out into traffic. My heart raced as we sped through the streets of central Moscow. A few minutes later we stood at the entrance to the Kremlin, an imposing compound with several buildings, colorful Moorish domes, and pink stone walls. It was really quite impressive, like a castle from a demented fairytale.

Poppy made a beeline to a side entrance. I held tight onto her leash and followed. She would find Kitty. A guard stood on either side of an ornately carved door. Clifford spoke to them in broken Russian. The larger of the two shook his head. "*Nyet.*" They wouldn't let us in.

Poppy barked up at the guards.

"Our niece is lost somewhere inside," I said. It was almost the truth.

"*Nyet.*" The guard stepped in front of the door.

Poppy growled.

Curses. Now what?

"Come on, Poppy." I tugged on her leash. Reluctantly, she gave up and let me lead.

We retreated to a café across the street. What was plan B? I sat at a table near the window so I could watch the entrance. There must be a way to get inside. If only Clifford and Poppy weren't along, I might have been able to use my maid's outfit to get in as one of the cleaning crew.

Clifford ordered us two Russian coffees and a plate of cream. My eyes glued to the Kremlin, I hardly noticed when the waiter returned with the drinks. Still staring across the street, I sipped my foamy coffee. The familiar burn of alcohol. I should have known. Followed by bursts of almond and sweet cream. I licked the whipped cream off my lip. Not bad.

Clifford sat the plate on the floor and Poppy lapped up the cream. If the waitstaff minded, they didn't say anything. Probably used to barmy British men feeding their spoiled little dogs cream from a plate.

"Look!" I pointed. "Isn't that Kitty?"

Clifford leaned across the table for a better view. "By Jove, you're right." He drained the last of his drink and then pulled a few notes from his wallet. "Waiter." He glanced around, looking for the waiter. "I'll just get change."

"Just leave it." I was already up with my gloves on, and Poppy's leash wrapped around my palm. "We don't have time." I snatched the notes from his hand and dropped them on the table. "Come on."

We hurried out of the café. I had to hold Poppy back from crossing the busy street in front of traffic. Finally, the traffic cleared, and we had our chance. We dashed across the street. "Where did she go?" I looked up and down the street. "Blast."

Poppy tugged at the leash. I had no choice but to let her lead. I slipped along behind her, trying not to fall.

"Where in blazes are you going?" Clifford rushed to catch up.

"To find Kitty." Poppy-poo knew where she was going. "I hope."

Poppy trotted around the corner and up the next street. Then she took off at a full gallop. I struggled to keep up. We dashed this way and that for another ten minutes. We'd twisted and turned so many times I doubted I could find my way back. Finally, the little beast skidded to a stop in front of a brownstone building. Clifford and I looked at each other. I scanned the list of names of the occupants.

What was the name of Kitty's old schoolmate? I ran my finger down the list. Abaza, Adamov, Alexandrov, Babushkin, Makarov. Surnames. Concentrate, Fiona. What was the name? I examined the initials of the missing first names. O. Alexandrov caught my eye. O for Olga. I pressed the doorbell. Nothing. I pressed it again. I could feel my pulse pounding in my neck. Kitty must be here. Otherwise, why did Poppy bring us here? I pressed the bell again.

"Sorry, old bean." Clifford rubbed his hands together. "Looks like we've lost her."

"She probably went back to the consulate." I shook my head. "At least we know she's okay." What about the rest of the ambassadors? What about Archie? A stabbing pain struck my chest. "Should we try to hail another taxicab?" My cheeks were stinging, and my fingers were numb. I promised myself once I knew Kitty and Archie were safe, I'd get a much-needed bath and a nice hot cuppa.

Clifford and I trudged down the street. Poppy yipped and yapped and tugged at the leash. "Settle down." I stopped and bent to pat her topknot. "Don't worry. We'll find her."

"Aunt Fiona?" The familiar voice came from behind us.

I spun around. "Kitty, dear."

Poppy bolted. The leash whiplashed. I opened my palm to let go. Even with my gloves on, it cut into my hand.

"Kitty, am I glad to see you." I pressed my good hand against the cut. "One of the ambassadors is a mole."

Kitty scooped up the dog and came to my side. Poppy licked her face. "I know." She leveled her gaze. "Aunt Fiona, I'm afraid I have some bad news."

My heart sank. I knew what she was going to say. Archie.

"Why don't you come inside?" She took my arm. "Olga can make us some tea."

Olga Alexandrov was a wiry young woman with jet-black hair and pale, almost translucent skin. She let us into her flat but wasn't exactly welcoming. No smiles. No chit-chat. Barely any eye-contact. She seemed especially suspicious of Poppy. Not that I blamed her. The dog was called Poppy-poo for a reason.

Olga's flat was modest in every way—size, furnishings, decorations. The bare walls and neat-as-a-pin kitchen suggested she didn't spend much time there. Did she have a boyfriend? A girlfriend? A job as a traveling salesperson? If she went to the same "boarding school" in France as Kitty, then she was probably a trained assassin.

Kitty invited us to sit around a table in an alcove off the kitchen that was set up as a dining room. I fidgeted in my chair, waiting for tea and the rest of Kitty's story about Archie. Was he dead? My stomach dropped like a trap door. I swallowed hard.

"Are you alright, Aunt Fiona?" Kitty asked. "You've gone white as a ghost."

"Tell us what happened…" I sucked in air. "To Archie."

"He knew what he was getting into when he signed up." Kitty's tone was defensive.

Surely it was more complicated. Most of the boys at the front had no idea what they were getting into before they went. I could tell by their faces when they arrived shot up and broken at Charing Cross Hospital. "Is he... de—" I couldn't say it out loud.

"I don't know." Kitty gave me her back and went to help Olga in the kitchen.

"What's that all about?" Clifford asked.

"You've got me." Was Archie dead or not? And why was Kitty acting so strange? What did she mean she didn't know?

Beads of sweat formed on my temples.

"Did the ambassadors succeed then?" Clifford pulled his pipe from his jacket pocket. "Maybe you were wrong, old girl." He nodded at me. "There was no mole." He struck a match and put it in the bowl.

"I'm right and Kitty confirmed." Now who sounded defensive? I felt like marching into the kitchen, grabbing the girl by the collar, and sitting her down. Why was she being so coy? Lives were at stake. And not just any lives. My fiancé's. Ex-fiancé. Alright. *Almost* ex-fiancé.

When Kitty returned with the tea tray, I demanded she tell us what had happened. Her defiant tone melted away as she recounted the ordeal.

"Archie is trapped in a trunk full of bullet holes?" I couldn't believe my ears. "How could you leave him there?" I was too upset to control my accusatory tone.

"Now, now, old thing," Clifford said, his pipe clamped between his teeth. "No reason to blame Kitty."

"There was nothing I could do for him." Kitty slumped in the chair. "My mission requires me to report back. And since one of the ambassadors has turned, I couldn't trust any one of them. I had to tell the War Office that we have a double agent."

"Well done, you." Clifford smiled at her.

"Speaking of double agents..." I proceeded to tell her about

Iron Victor and his nocturnal meetings. "I tried to get back in time to warn you." I blew on my tea. "To warn all of you." My hand trembled as I raised the cup to my lips.

"Someone killed Iron Victor because he knew about Operation Ambassadors." Kitty frowned. "The killer is one of ours. But who?"

"If one of ours killed Iron Victor for the sake of Operation Ambassadors," I sipped my tea, "then why did he let you walk into the trap? Why didn't he warn you?"

"Maybe he didn't have time." Olga joined the conversation. "You say Victor died early this morning. By then the plan was already underway."

"I say." Clifford's eyes lit up. "Maybe someone did for the killer too and he didn't make it out alive."

Was it possible there could be another body in the house or on the grounds of Iron Victor's place? I rehearsed the suspects. The countess. The mystery man. And Fredricks. Good grief. What if Clifford was right, and Fredricks murdered Iron Victor, and then someone killed him? Archie and Fredricks both gone. It was unbearable.

"Who do you make as the mole?" I asked Kitty. At least if Archie gave his life for the mission, it wasn't him. "Not Archie."

She nodded. "Not Archie."

"That leaves Lockhart, Reilly, and Savinkov." Clifford counted them off on his fingers. "Lockhart and Reilly are true blue British patriots."

"Reilly escaped through the window." Kitty buttoned the top button of her dress. "He bailed out as soon as the shooting started. And the Cheka let him go. No one went after him."

"So, you think Reilly is the mole?" I peered over the lip of my teacup.

"Possible." She thought for a minute. "Savinkov isn't above

suspicion either. No one has seen him since the botched operation."

"And Sir Robert Lockhart?" I asked.

"He's a good man." Clifford clamped his pipe between his teeth. "I knew his father. The senior Lockhart and I used to hunt together. He was a mensch. And a darned good shot."

I held up my hand before he really got going. "You don't think the mole and Iron Victor's killer could be one and the same man?"

"Why would a mole for the Bolsheviks, or their double agent, kill the chief of the secret police?" Kitty shook her head. "The Cheka is the enforcer for the Bolsheviks. They work hand in glove."

She had a point. If the police and the mole both worked for the Bolsheviks, then they would be on the same side and the mole would have no reason to kill the chief of police. At least not an official reason. A personal reason, perhaps? Right now, I didn't care about the relationship between the Cheka and the Bolsheviks. All I cared about was my relationship with Archie. "What about Archie?" I bit my lip.

"What about him?" Kitty stared into her teacup as if she'd find the answer at the bottom of the cup.

"Shouldn't we go back for him?" Tears welled in my eyes. "Maybe he's still alive and trapped in that trunk." How awful. My stomach flipped. Like being buried alive. If it was riddled with bullet holes, at least he wouldn't suffocate.

"My uncle works at the Kremlin as a codebreaker." Olga tossed her long hair over one shoulder. "I might be able to find out from him."

"Would he tell us?" I narrowed my brows. Why would a Soviet codebreaker help British agents, especially since they'd just tried to kill the Bolshevik leader?

"For a price." Olga smiled. "He's loyal to the tsar and hates the communists. But he's also xenophobic"—she shrugged—"and no fan of the British."

"What price?" I sat blinking at her. I was a mere file clerk turned spy, hardly a princess.

"He loves your thick-cut orange marmalade." She winked.

"That's it?" I smiled weakly. "He'd do it for marmalade?" Come to think of it, marmalade wasn't easy to come by these days. Bloody war. The only person I knew who could get his hands on real orange marmalade was Fredrick Fredricks. The rest of us had to settle for that awful stuff made from carrots.

"And..." Olga stood up. "Help us scotch the White Rose Directive."

Good heavens. She knew about the White Rose Directive. "The Cheka's plans for the royal family?"

"Yes." Her eyes went wide. "How do you know about it?"

"My night spent under Iron Victor's desk." I shifted in my chair. I wasn't sure how much I trusted Kitty's school chum.

Olga nodded as if she'd spent many a night there herself. "Now they'll execute the royal family in retaliation for the assassination of Victor." She gritted her teeth. "They're ruthless." Her eyes hardened like two black diamonds.

"Good lord." Clifford removed the pipe from his mouth. "Execute?"

"Until they dispose of every last nobleman, the tsarists will still have reason to fight." Olga balled up her fists.

"Only by cutting off its head," Kitty said with a faraway look in her eyes, "can we stop the beast."

"If they execute the royal family..." Of course. "The tsarists lose their purpose." A light bulb went off in my brain. "No tsar, no tsarists."

13

PLAN B

We were still at Olga's flat. It had been almost two hours. My grumbling stomach told me I was overdue for lunch. By the time Olga reached her uncle, I was on my fifth cup of strong Russian tea. My nerves were live wires. My hands trembled as I finished the last cup. The flat was so chilly that I was tempted to have another to warm up but thought better of it. My pulse was already racing; whether from the tea or worrying about Archie, I couldn't be sure.

Clifford, Kitty, Poppy, and I waited in the sitting area, while in the kitchen, Olga talked to her uncle.

"Don't worry, old girl." Clifford reached over and patted my hand.

Was it that obvious? I fiddled with my teacup. "With every passing hour, the chances of saving Archie diminish." If he wasn't dead already.

"If that trunk is made of steel, he's well protected." Clifford puffed his pipe. "I've seen steel tanks take a shelling and come out without a dent. Why, I remember at the Battle of Cambrai before I was shot up." He tapped his bad knee. "Colonel Fuller and the

Tank Corps ran right over the Germans. Bloody brass didn't exploit the victory and instead followed up with the horse calvary when he should have brought more indestructible tanks." He shook his head and took another drag off his pipe. "Then there was the time—"

"Yes, Clifford, dear." I patted his arm. "Thank you. Steel is strong stuff." Usually his nattering on annoyed me, but I had to admit his story about the tanks was reassuring. Maybe Archie did survive. And yet, by now, surely the Cheka had dragged him away, dead or alive. I squeezed my eyes shut. "We can't just leave him there." My voice cracked.

"So, you do love him." Kitty tilted her head, giving me a knowing look.

Did I? My heart ached imagining losing him. I'd already lost so much. But did that mean I loved him?

"After we rescue him, you should marry him and get it over with." Kitty stroked the sleeping pup, who was curled up on her lap.

"*If* we rescue him." I shuddered to think what had become of him.

"He could still be alive." Kitty adjusted the dog's bow. "I *took care* of the Cheka." She winked. "I even delayed the backup squad." She gave me a reassuring smile. "They couldn't have known he was hiding in the trunk."

"Trapped in a trunk." I shuddered. Even with air-holes, how long could he last in a trunk? Especially if he'd been shot.

"Archie is a good agent and a good man." She patted my hand. "He's probably at a pub having drinks with Reilly and Savinkov." She smiled.

"Yes, he is a good man." I squeezed her hand. It was true. Archie was a good agent and a good man and as such he would not be having cocktails with traitors like Reilly and Savinkov.

Fredricks's protestations to the contrary, I didn't believe for a moment that Archie was a double agent.

"You should marry him." Kitty met my gaze. "You know he loves you."

Just because I didn't want the man dead didn't mean I wanted to marry him. "Why are you in such a hurry to marry me off?" I squinted at her. I'd been married once, and it turned out a disaster. I wasn't in a rush to try it again.

Kitty glanced at Clifford and then turned back to me. "You know why."

Sigh. Fredricks. She didn't approve. Who would? He was an enemy spy. And he'd lured me here and then abandoned me to the Bolsheviks. The rotter.

Finally, Olga returned. "My uncle heard about the attack at the Kremlin." She sat down on the sofa next to Kitty. "The Cheka arrested Robert Lockhart. He's being held in the central jail."

"Did they find Reilly?" Kitty rearranged Poppy, who was asleep and sliding off her lap.

"Sidney Reilly got away." Olga raised her eyebrows.

"And Boris Savinkov?" Kitty asked.

"No sign of him." Olga blinked. "Convenient, don't you think?"

"A little too convenient." Kitty nodded.

"What about Archie?" I was afraid to ask.

"My uncle doesn't know what happened to—"

"Did they find..." I winced, "a body?"

"Several." Olga winked at Kitty. "Four Cheka guards shot dead and another one wounded." She smiled. "He tripped loading the ambassador into a police lorry. Broke his foot." Olga may not be warm and welcoming, but she kept a cool head. I liked that about her.

"We need a plan." I pulled my notebook from my skirt pocket.

"How will we get into the Kremlin?" My pencil hovering over the pad, I searched the faces of my friends. "Any ideas?"

"My uncle told me a special meeting of all security staff is scheduled for five o'clock this afternoon." Olga smiled. "While the guards are getting chewed out, we can sneak in."

"Surely, not all the guards." I wrote five o'clock on my pad.

"Skeleton staff only." Olga's voice was full of excitement. "And a special crew is coming to clean and repair the damage in the office." She was the most animated she'd been since we'd arrived.

"So, we blend in with that crew." Kitty slapped the table and Poppy squeaked. "Sorry, Poppy-poo." She settled the pup back into her lap.

Clifford's eyes lit up. "I say, breaking into the Kremlin."

"Not breaking into the Kremlin." Olga's countenance turned serious again. "The cleaning company is called Petrov and we'll need to infiltrate their office and procure uniforms."

"Breaking into Petrov's." I blinked. Breaking and entering. I hoped to heaven we didn't all end up in a Russian jail. Setting pencil to paper, I made a note:

Break into Petrov's. Steal uniforms. Save Archie. Five o'clock.

I glanced at my watch. "We have three hours. We'd better get to it." Trouble was, now we needed a plan to break into Petrov's. I turned to Olga. "I don't suppose you know anyone at this Petrov's?"

"As a matter of fact, a friend of my brother's girlfriend has a cousin who works there."

"Of course he does." I'd never met anyone so well-connected in my life.

"Uncle Clifford could pretend to be an inspector and grab the uniforms." Kitty looked to him. "How's your Russian?"

"Not up to snuff, I'm afraid." He sighed. "I can order my lunch and find the loo, but not much more." He shrugged and went back to puffing like a chimney.

"You and Olga are fluent." I sat on my hands to keep from fidgeting. "Can't one of you—"

"Despite the Bolsheviks and their ideals of equality," Olga scoffed, "no one would believe a woman was an inspector."

"Unlike you, Aunt Fiona, some of us can't pass as men no matter how hard we try." Kitty grinned. "And, since you sound like you're reading from the dictionary when you speak Russian, we need a plan B."

"I bet I know someone." I stood up and took my cup and saucer to the kitchen. The question was, could I find him and persuade him to help me rescue Archie? He wasn't a fan of the lieutenant. And as far as Archie was concerned, they were engaged in a fight to the death. And not just over national allegiances. No. For Archie it was personal. Fredricks laughed it off— but he would have killed Archie long ago if it wasn't for me. Now that he was going around with the countess, perhaps the cad had forgotten about me. Natasha was beautiful and charming, in a predatory way. Fredricks was used to being the predator—the panther—and not the prey. "We need to get to the Metropol Hotel."

"You can't be serious." Kitty joined me in the kitchen. Poppy trotted behind her mistress. "Really, Aunt Fiona." She scowled at me. "I know what you're thinking and it's a terrible idea."

"But he can help us." I took a sponge to my dishes. "And we need orange marmalade."

"Why?" Kitty put her hands on her hips. "Why would he help his enemy?"

"Because he cares for me." My cheeks burned.

"That's what he wants you to think." She rolled her eyes. "He's manipulating you."

"No. He's genuine." The heat spread down my neck.

"It's a performance." Kitty shook her head. "He's a good actor."

"We'll see." I placed the clean dishes in the rack. "What could it hurt?"

"Ah. Let's see… we could be captured and killed." She raised her voice. "We could be tortured until we betray state secrets."

"State secrets." I chuckled. "All they could get out of me is Captain Hall's nickname. I don't know anything else."

"Excuse me." Kitty looked incredulous. "Miss Photographic Memory. You know the entire contents of top-secret files in Room 40. Why do you think Fredricks wants to get close to you?"

I hunched over like a deflated balloon. Maybe she was right. Fredricks wanted me to access secret files. Yes. I could recreate those files, even if I didn't know what half of them meant. But Fredricks had never asked me to betray state secrets. He was always a perfect gentleman. Even that time I'd had too much wine… and kissed him. Warmth spread further down. I looked away. "I'm using him just as much as he's using me."

"Oh, really." She laughed. "And what top-secret intel have you gotten out of him?"

"He helped negotiate the peace treaty between the Bolsheviks and the Germans." I glanced at her to gauge her reaction.

"He did?" She squinted at me. "So that's why he's here." Aha. She didn't know.

"He is—er, was—involved with Iron Victor and visited his house regularly." I didn't mention that Fredricks never told me any of this himself.

"What makes you think he isn't the one who informed on the ambassadors?" Her gaze was piercing.

"How could he have known about Operation Ambassadors?" I rinsed the last cup and put it in the rack.

"Do you talk in your sleep?" Cheeky girl.

"Of course not." I flicked the dish towel for effect.

"How do you know *Fredricks* didn't kill Iron Victor?"

"I don't." I folded the towel and hung it over the tap. "All the more reason to find the bounder and see what he knows."

"And you think he's going to tell you?" Kitty shook her head. "Aunt Fiona, you need to stop being so gullible."

"And you need to stop being so impudent." I slid past her and left the kitchen. At the threshold, I turned back. "Do you have a better idea?"

"I wish I did." She followed me out into the sitting room and then announced, "We're going to the Metropol."

* * *

The hotel had transformed overnight. A makeshift banner covered the entrance. It read, *Second House of the Soviets*. Armed guards patrolled the lobby. Suspicious-looking men, no doubt Cheka, peeked up over newspapers and smoked cigarettes behind potted ferns. Ivan the porter was nowhere to be seen. And the reception desk was manned by a uniformed officer of the Red Army.

Olga took the lead. As a French operative who had infiltrated the Cheka, hopefully she knew what to do. The rest of us lagged behind as she approached the desk. She and the attendant exchanged a few words and then she produced an identification card. The officer was not impressed by her credentials. He shook his head. Olga raised her voice. The officer didn't budge.

"Excuse me, sir." I stepped up to the desk. "I'm a friend, a *very good* friend, of Duke Pavel Zakrevsky." I smiled. "He's expecting me."

The officer gave me a quizzical look. Olga translated for me. Whatever she said, the man's countenance brightened and the smile on his face was like sunshine after a rainstorm. He came out from behind the desk and made a gesture for me to follow him. Reluctantly, Kitty agreed to let me go alone while she, Clifford, and Olga waited in the lobby.

I fell in behind the officer. He led me up the stairs to suite 315. So, Fredricks had returned to the suite. Good. The officer knocked on the door and then smiled back at me. Suddenly, I had butterflies in my stomach. I hadn't seen Fredricks since London. And he hadn't exactly gone out of his way to find me in Moscow. I patted my wig, cleared my throat, and took a deep breath.

The moment of truth. Would Fredricks greet me as a beloved friend or an enemy spy? If Kitty was right, how would I tell the difference?

True, Fredricks was a master of disguise. And he was devilishly clever and a cad. Probably a womanizer and a killer of double agents. He had tricked me in the past. Like when he pretended that I'd shot him so he could escape in Austria. Or when he stole my nun's habit and tied me up in Paris. But those passionate kisses in Italy and then again in London. No. I refused to believe his tenderness was a performance. He cooked for me, for heaven's sake. And then those extravagant flowers when I first arrived. Surely I couldn't be such a dupe.

Footfalls from inside the suite. Fredricks was on the other side of the door. The click of the lock. My cheeks warmed. The door opened.

"Duke Zakrevsky." The officer greeted the man and then pointed to me. "I bring English wife," he said in broken English.

Wife! Had Olga told him I was the duke's wife?

I did a double take. The man standing before me wore tan jodhpurs, a white blouse and wool hunting jacket, and tall black boots. Long black hair flowed out from under a slouch hat. He was a big man, like Fredricks.

But not Fredricks.

Indeed, with his red nose and giant mole, he looked nothing like Fredricks. Who was this imposter posing as Fredricks pretending to be a Russian duke? Flustered, I held out my hand. "Glad to meet you."

The officer tilted his head and gave me a curious look.

"I've missed you, my dear." I feigned a smile, hoping the officer would leave us alone so I could find out what the heck was going on. I turned to the officer. "Thank you, sir."

The imposter said something, and the officer turned on his heels and disappeared back down the hall. When he was out of earshot, I leveled my gaze. "Who are you and what have you done with Fredricks?"

14

DUKE ZAKREVSKY

The imposter denied knowing anyone named Fredrick Fredricks. He claimed he'd found the clothes in the closet, left by the last tenant of the suite. He insisted he was the real Duke Zakrevsky. When I asked why the Bolsheviks allowed an aristocrat to stay at the Metropol, he shrugged and said, "I'm a friend."

Whose friend? The Bolsheviks'? Or Fredricks's? When I asked to inspect his suite, he balked. Huffing and puffing, he called me "offensive." Obviously, I wouldn't get any information out of this imposter, so I returned to my own friends.

My mind racing, I descended the stairs. Where was Fredricks? Had he been kidnapped or arrested or worse? I glanced at my watch. And what would we do now? We had no plan B and our window for infiltrating the special cleaning crew was closing. How would we get into the Kremlin and find Archie? What a mess.

"There was a man in suite 315 and he was wearing Fredricks's clothes, but he wasn't Fredricks." I told my friends what had happened.

"Big man with a bulbous nose and a hairy mole?" Kitty asked.

"How did you know?" My eyes went wide. Did she know him?

"Latvian baker here to visit his daughter." She sighed. "I met him before."

"He claims to be the real Duke Zakrevsky."

"I say." Clifford puffed his pipe. "Sounds like a bit of a sticky wicket."

"We need a new plan." My stomach growled, reminding me I hadn't eaten yet today. Given my nerves, I couldn't eat. But I could do with a cup of tea. I remembered a café across the street. "Mind if we grab a cuppa and figure out plan C?"

My friends and I reconvened at a nearby eatery. Praga restaurant occupied a quaint two-story rounded corner building. The curtained windows of the upper floor each had their own framing columns with ornate awnings and starburst patterns. Inside, long tables covered in white linen set with crystal glasses were the last remnants of elite dining in Soviet-controlled Russia. A waiter showed us to a table near a window that looked out over Red Square. From the first floor, we had a tremendous view of the Kremlin and beyond.

Olga ordered *Sbiten* to warm us up, along with something called *Shuba*. As we waited for our drinks to arrive, we plotted our next step. My plan to enlist Fredricks had failed. And we were running out of time if we wanted to sneak into the Kremlin with the special cleaning crew.

The waiter arrived with the *Sbiten*, which turned out to be a delightful warm honey drink. A minute later he returned with plates heaped with potatoes, carrots, eggs, and beets in a white sauce. Then he sat a plate of *Shuba* in front of each of us.

"What is it?" I asked, suspicious of new foodstuffs, especially those covered in unknown sauces. Give me plain toast and tea any day.

"Looks delicious." Clifford took a forkful. A culinary adventurer, he was always ready to try something new.

Kitty pushed a potato with her knife, revealing some sort of fish underneath.

"Herring under a fur coat." Olga took a bite.

"I beg your pardon?" Herring? Fur coat? Didn't sound appetizing.

Olga smiled. "That's what *Shuba* means. The fur coat." She held up a forkful. "Because of the meat shortage, Soviets promote eating fish." She popped the bite into her mouth. "At first, canned herring was a hard sell." She took another bite. "Until the Bolshevik minister of food pulled a pearl necklace from a can and claimed smugglers hid jewels inside." She grinned. "Now tinned fish is very popular."

I took a tiny bite of potatoes. Hmm. The white sauce wasn't bad.

"Excuse me." Another waiter appeared at my side. "Miss, may I have a word?"

What in the world?

"In private?" He glanced over at my friends.

What would a waiter want with me? I stared up into his face, searching for the answer. Oh, my word. Those mischievous dark eyes, the dimples, the black hair tucked up into a white cap. The broad shoulders and narrow waist around which his apron was tied. The gold pinky ring sporting a panther insignia was the final proof. Fredrick Fredricks. "What are you doing here?" I hissed.

He gestured with his head toward an alcove near the lavatories. "Not here," he whispered.

"Excuse me." I dropped my napkin on the table and stood up.

"I say, what's going on?" Clifford jumped up, always ready to defend a woman in trouble.

"It's okay, Clifford dear." I patted his arm. "I know him."

"You do?" He sat back down, a confused look on his face.

"So do you." Obviously, he didn't recognize Fredricks.

"Mind yourself, Aunt Fiona." Kitty gave me a knowing look. She had recognized the bounder.

Ignoring us completely, Olga continued devouring her herring in a fur coat.

I followed Fredricks to the alcove. "Why are you disguised as a waiter? Who is that man in your suite? Where have you been? Why weren't you here when I arrived?" The dam broke and questions rushed out like a raging river. "I thought you'd been kidnapped or worse." My lip trembled as I fought back tears.

"Slow down, ma chérie." He took my hand and kissed it. "I'm here now."

I yanked my hand away and folded my arms over my chest. *Too little, too late.* "So?"

"Now, now, Fiona. Don't be cross." Flashing white canines, he smiled down at me. "Although the flush in your cheeks when you're angry is very alluring." He lightly brushed a finger against my cheek. Soft as a feather.

I tightened my lips. I wasn't going to let him sweet talk me this time. I glared at him.

"Alright, alright." He sighed. "I had a disagreement with the head of the secret police. That's why I'm in disguise. And I'm here across from the hotel waiting for you. The man in my suite kindly agreed to act as a decoy, for a price, of course. I've been in Brest-Litovsk facilitating the peace talks. They took longer than expected and I couldn't get back in time to greet you." He bowed slightly. "For that, I'm deeply sorry." He took a step closer. So close, I could feel the warmth radiating from his body. And the scent of sandalwood and mustache wax and masculinity made my breath catch.

"Can you forgive me?" His whispered baritone sent shivers up my spine.

Why did he have to be so blasted attractive? I took a step backwards and ran into the wall. I was dizzy and felt like my knees might buckle. *Get a grip, Fiona. Now is not the time to swoon.* Not that I was one for swooning. Especially over Fredricks, the rogue. Steeling myself, I leaned into the wall for support. "There is something you could do." My voice cracked. "To redeem yourself."

"My love isn't redemption enough?" He unfolded my arms and took my hand. "Love is a priceless treasure. You can redeem the whole world by it, and cleanse not only your own sins but the sins of others."

"I'm not talking about sins... or love, for that matter." I didn't remove my hand. I should have, but I couldn't. The dry, smooth warmth of his palm was reassuring. I wished I could fit into that palm so he might carry me with him wherever he went.

"Dostoevsky. He believed any sin, even murder..." He paused and looked down at me, the spark in his mischievous eyes softening. "Could be redeemed by love."

"So that's it." I averted my gaze. "You want me to forgive you for murder." I suspected he'd poisoned the countess at Ravenswick Abbey and another in Paris. Both supposedly double agents who'd turned from spying for Germany to spying for us. Fredricks always maintained they were the most dangerous because they knew all the Germans' secrets. And for that reason, they had to be dispatched.

"And I suppose you and Iron Victor disagreed over your interpretation of Dostoevsky." I snorted. *Disagreement, my eye. Murder more like.*

"True. Victor's tastes in Russian literature and mine do

diverge. He prefers Tolstoy and finds Dostoevsky dark and self-indulgent—"

"Dark and self-indulgent sounds right up your alley." My tone was too playful for an interrogation into murder. But I couldn't help it. Paradoxically, Fredricks was both disarming and suspicious.

"Ma chérie." He gave my hand a squeeze. "How well you know me."

Kitty poked her head around the corner.

I quickly withdrew my hand from Fredricks's.

She gave me a dirty look. "If you're done playing pattycakes, maybe you want to get back to rescuing your fiancé?"

"We're not playing pattycakes and he's not my fiancé." I looked at Fredricks. Why were *his* cheeks pink? Nothing embarrassed him. Wait. Was he suppressing laughter? I leveled my gaze at him. "Will you help us or not?"

"You're no longer engaged to the dashing young Lieutenant Somersby?" he asked, mirth dripping from his lips.

"What's so blasted funny?" I stomped my foot. "Archie could be dead, for heaven's sake."

"Who called it off?" His eyes sparkled. "You or him?"

"What difference does it make?" Archie had basically given me an ultimatum. Marry him on the spot or never. Since I couldn't marry him on the spot, the default was never. Right now, I just wanted him alive. Fiancé or not. "The point is, we need to rescue him, if he's still..."

"All the difference in the world," Fredricks interrupted.

"Are we going after Archie or not?" Kitty asked, her hands on her hips. The silly schoolgirl had transformed into the bossy assassin. I wasn't sure which one I preferred.

"I heard your lieutenant got caught in a rather unpleasant

situation this morning." He sighed. "Let me guess. That's how I can redeem myself? Help you retrieve your young man?"

I nodded.

"You know I'll do anything for you." He reached for my hand again, but I was too quick. "You only have to ask." He tucked a stray lock of wig hair behind my ear. "Although I've warned you about the good lieutenant. He's not what he seems. And he's boring to boot." He shrugged. "But if he makes you happy—"

"Stop the sentimental drivel." Kitty cut him off. "And quit trying to confuse her." She took my elbow. "Come on, Aunt Fiona. Let's go."

"Ahh. Our little Miss Kitty is growing up." Fredricks chuckled. "And so is her temper." He took hold of my other elbow. "I will help you save your erstwhile fiancé."

With him pulling one way and Kitty the other, I felt like a rope in a tug-o-war. He let go of my arm and took the lead, before adding, "Even if the rake plans to shoot me on sight."

* * *

The friend of the brother of a cousin delivered the uniforms for Petrov's special cleaning crew. Olga didn't want Fredricks in her flat. In fact, she refused to speak to him. So, we met the friend at a bombed-out church next to the Kremlin. Afternoon light streamed in through broken stained-glass windows, fracturing the otherwise dark cathedral. Biblical scenes frescoed on the walls were pocked with bullet holes. The altar was in shambles, with overturned offering cups and a smashed communion chalice. A decanter still filled with wine made it look as if the priests had simply disappeared during a ceremony. Once filled with the scent of incense and the warmth of communion, now the abandoned church was cold and drafty and smelled of mildew with rodent signs in every corner. Not the most comfortable place to change clothes. But we had no time to lose.

Seemingly out of thin air, Fredricks had produced a lorry with "Petrov's" freshly painted across both sides. How did he do it? More to the point, *why* did he do it? How could helping his enemy be part of a performance? Fredricks emerged from the shadows. Hair pulled back, and wearing coveralls, a newsboy cap, and a fake beard, he looked every bit the foreman of a special cleaning crew. The sleeves of his rough shirt were rolled up to reveal smooth, muscular forearms. "I'll go fetch the lorry and bring it around." Fredricks took off at a trot.

The rest of the crew looked the part, too. Except for Clifford. The trouser legs and shirt sleeves were too short and, like a scarecrow, his lanky frame stuck out in every direction.

"Clifford, dear." I pointed to where his arm protruded from his sleeve. "Why don't you and Poppy wait in the lorry?"

He got that sad hangdog look of his.

"You can stand guard and give a signal if the Cheka arrive," I added, hoping an important-sounding assignment would cheer him up.

His countenance brightened. "Poppy makes a jolly good watchdog."

"Where *is* Poppy?" Frantically, Kitty dashed around the abandoned building calling for her pup.

Poppy barked. It sounded far away and echoed through the church. I hated to think what the little beast had gotten into. Clifford and I joined the search while Olga leaned against a pillar, watching from the sidelines.

"Behind the altar," Clifford called out.

From the other side of the church, Kitty took off running.

I followed the sound of the barking. Sure enough, it was coming from behind the altar. Stepping over pieces of plaster and debris, I made my way around to the back. Even with my head start, Kitty beat me to it. She and Clifford stood by watching while Poppy desperately scratched at an ornate, carved wooden door.

"What's she on about?" I joined them. "She's making claw marks on that beautiful door."

"Look around, Aunt Fiona." Kitty's tone was sharp. "The place is already a ruin."

"I say. Do you think I should open the door?" Clifford lit a match and held it close to the door.

"Listen. Do you hear something?" I went to Clifford's side and put my ear to the door. I could barely make out a low moaning on the other side. "Good heavens. Someone's in there."

Clifford turned the doorknob. "Locked, I'm afraid."

"Give me some light." Kitty wedged in front of him.

He lit another match and held it out. With the dexterity of a magician pulling a sleight of hand, Kitty maneuvered a rake and wrench until the lock clicked. I envied her lockpick set. And her expertise. Compared to her, I was an amateur. She turned the knob and opened the door a few inches. "Something's blocking the door."

The pup squeezed through the crack. "What do you see?" Kitty asked. Did she think the dog could answer her?

Poppy squeaked. All I could see of her was her tail wagging.

"Popster, am I glad to see you." The voice was weak, but unmistakable. "Kitty, is that you?"

"Archie." I knelt, clasped my hands together in prayer, and then peered through the crack. "We're here."

15

LIFE OR DEATH

The others went to find Fredricks and the lorry and to fetch a stretcher and some tools to remove the door. I stayed with Archie. He had lost so much blood that he was fading in and out of consciousness. His body blocked the door, but he couldn't manage to move. The heavy skirt of my Petrov uniform tucked under me, I sat on the filthy floor and leaned against the wall, peering into the crack. The door was opened just enough that I could make out Archie's outline in the dim light coming from the broken church windows on the other side of the altar. I reached through the opening and took his hand. It was hot and damp. The hand of a feverish man.

"What happened?" I peered through the crack, waiting for my eyes to adjust.

"I'm shot." He wheezed. "I escaped through Lenin's secret panel." His breath was labored. "It led me here, but the door was locked. If you hadn't found me..." His voice trailed off.

"Secret panel?" What was he talking about?

"They were ready." He was panting now. "They knew."

"It was a trap." Despite the cold, beads of perspiration formed on my forehead. "I came to warn you. But I was too late." If only I could have warned him in time.

He moaned. "Fiona..."

"Don't talk." What could I do to help him? There must be something. "Save your strength." Where were they? Waiting for the others to get back was torment.

"I'm sorry." He sounded miles away.

"It's not your fault." Through the crack, I squeezed his hand. "There's a mole in the—"

"No. Not that." He cut me off, a new urgency in his voice. "I should have agreed to wait like you asked. I was a stubborn ass. Fiona, I'm sorry. You know you're my best girl." His words were coming fast, a torrent of remorse and longing. "And now I've lost you." He struggled to get the words out. "I'm an idiot."

"You're not an idiot." Standing on my knees, I stretched my arm through the opening until my fingertips brushed his cheek. "It's my fault. I should have—" Should have what? Married him on the spot? *Don't think of that now.* "Where are you shot?" I ripped at the hem of my skirt. "Can you make a tourniquet?"

"My arm and my side." He groaned again, as if talking about it was painful. "I tied a sock around my arm. But my side..."

"Here." I tore a long piece of fabric. "Hold this against your side." I handed it to him through the opening. How long had he been lying here bleeding? Kitty told me they'd been ambushed early this morning. I didn't need to look at my watch to know the sun was setting. The light in the church had turned the hazy violet of twilight. A winter sunset that was more lament than mad tuba.

A long silence. I leaned in to look through the crack. My heart leaped into my throat. In the dark, he looked like a pile of wet clothes.

He stirred. *Thank goodness.* "Water," he croaked.

Water? Where could I get some water? I glanced around. Wait. The sacramental wine in the crystal decanter on the altar. "Right away." I dashed around the altar, grabbed the wine, and skidded back around to the door. "Here." I slid the decanter through the opening. "Drink." I wished I could hold him in my arms and lift the bottle to his lips. *Oh, Archie. I'm the idiot. Not you. There must be something I can do.*

"Archie, remember Paris?" I could distract him until the others returned with a stretcher and tools to remove the door. "When we first kissed?" The memory flooded my chest.

"Your mustache tickled." He chuckled and then coughed.

I smiled. I'd been on assignment disguised as Harold the helpful bellboy. "How did you know it was me?"

"I'd know you anywhere." More coughing. "Those beautiful eyes. And you smell like springtime."

In my mind's eye I could see that irresistible lock of chestnut hair falling over his forehead. "And you smell like a cedar forest... and Kenilworths."

"You don't happen to have one?" His voice perked up. "My shot-up wing is useless. Can't twist it far enough to get in my own pocket."

"You know I don't smoke." At this moment, I sincerely wished I did smoke. At least then I could offer Archie some comfort.

"Right. A smashing girl like you would never." I could hear the wine sloshing. He must have taken a swig.

"Under the mistletoe in Cairo..." I closed my eyes and conjured that moment only months ago. If only we could go back to that embrace.

"Kitty interrupted my awkward proposal." The decanter clanked against the floor when he sat it down. "Probably just as well."

"I didn't think so." I tucked my knees up against my chin and hugged myself. "At the time, I wanted to throttle her."

"When I finally did get it out, you gutted me." He sounded defeated.

"I'm sorry." In Italy, when he'd dropped to one knee and proposed, I was overwhelmed. A man had died, for heaven's sake. And by then, I knew Archie was more than just a flyboy with the Royal Air Force. He was a spy. And not just a spy for the War Office. Something more. His missions were top-secret. He always knew more than I did and could never tell me even half. His whole life was classified. By then, I'd realized he was an assassin. I leaned my forehead against my knees. "I'm so, so sorry."

"I shouldn't have pressured you." The wine sloshed in the bottle again. Hopefully it was quenching his thirst and quelling his pain. "I behaved like a spoiled brat."

True. His behavior was childish. I still didn't understand why he was in such a hurry. Why couldn't we wait until after the war? Why had he insisted we get married that very day? The day I'd walked out on him and decided to follow Fredricks to Moscow. How I hoped he didn't know I'd come here for Fredricks. How I hoped he believed I was here on assignment.

"Let's not dwell on the past." I sighed. "Let's plan for the future." *Please, God, let him have a future.*

"What future?" His words were sharp. "I don't think—" He sucked in air.

"Our future." I squinted to see through the opening. The dim light reflecting off his eyes, wide and wild. A strange gurgling sound made me grimace.

"Fiona." His voice was barely audible, a thread of sound vibrating between life and death.

I leaned forward and reached through the opening. My fingertips brushing his cheek again. Or was it his arm? "Stay with

me, Archie." *Oh, please, God, don't let him die. Please save him.*
Silently, I prayed. I prayed hard. Maybe in this church God would
hear me. I wished I was a true believer. A woman of faith.
Growing up on my grandparents' farm, I'd learned to put my
faith in the soil and the sun and the rain. Never bothering about a
higher power. "Archie?"

"Don't leave me," he gasped.

"I won't." I bit my lip, choking back tears. "Never."

His head fell against my hand, tugging at the ligaments in my
forearm. A pain shot up my arm. I withdrew it and fell back on
my haunches. Where were Clifford and Kitty? Why weren't they
back yet? *Come on, people. He's dying.* I listened for his jagged
breath. Nothing. The uncanny stillness made me shudder.

"Archie?"

No response. The silence was deafening. I wanted to scream.

"Archie? Can you hear me?" I had a sick feeling. He was
unconscious. Or was he—? No. He couldn't be.

Why in blazes hadn't I married him when he asked? Now he
was going to die, and I couldn't even hold him in my arms. I
closed my eyes and brushed tears from my cheeks with the backs
of my hands. "Oh, Archie, don't die," I whispered through my
tears. *Please, God. If you save him, I promise I'll marry him whenever
he wants.* On hands and knees, I peered through the opening. If
only I had my torch. I couldn't tell whether he was breathing.

This bloody war. So much death. And why? Land? What good
was land if you were dead? Honor? No. War was not honorable.
I'd seen too much suffering and pain to believe that lie. All those
broken men, some of them no more than boys. None of us would
ever be the same. Even if we survived this bloody war. I buried my
face in my hands and let out a silent scream. Why? What good
did it do to sacrifice the best of us?

"Archie?" I sniffed. "Can you hear me?" I listened.

Windswept pebbles tapping against a broken window. Curtains flapping under the altar table. Motorcars passing outside. A man shouting in Russian. The sounds of life indifferent to our presence. They would go on without us. I collapsed back against the wall. The stone was cold against my shoulder blades. I tried to conjure the cedar forest and those sea-green eyes. I couldn't. Instead, the metallic smell of blood filled my nostrils. And when I closed my eyes, all I saw was that pile of wet clothes.

I pressed my palms together. "Please. I'll do anything," I whispered into my clasped hands. "I promise." I turned my gaze to skyward. "If you save him..."

"Fiona." A sound so faint I wondered if I was hallucinating. "Fiona."

"I'm here." I shook tears away and knelt by the door. "I'm here, Archie." I put my hand through the crack and recoiled at the dampness. I jerked my hand back. Red. Blood. "What's taking so long?" I shouted into the darkness. My voice echoed through the empty church. "Where the hell are you?"

"We're here." Kitty's voice was a tonic for my tortured soul.

"Hurry." I wiped my hand on my skirt. Using the wall for support, I stood up. My stiff legs wobbled. I was light-headed. "Get him out of there."

Clifford and Fredricks carried a stretcher loaded with equipment while Kitty held up a saw and a sledgehammer. Olga must have had enough because she was nowhere to be seen.

"Olga had to report for work," Kitty said, as if reading my mind. "She's undercover in the Cheka."

I nodded and took the sledgehammer from her hand. Ouch. It dropped and banged against my leg. It was heavier than I'd anticipated. I grabbed it and made to swing.

"Wait." Fredricks lit a lantern. "Let's not panic." He came to my side and took the sledgehammer. "Best to take out the hinges and remove the door carefully, especially if the good lieutenant is on the other side."

"I'm not sure he's still alive." My lip trembled.

"Don't worry, ma chérie." Fredricks wiped a tear from my cheek. "We'll save your lad." He handed me a handkerchief. "I won't let him die."

"I don't think it's up to you." I dabbed at my eyes.

"We'll see about that. Stand clear." Fredricks raised the sledgehammer and brought it down on one of the hinges with such force that the ancient metal cracked. Two pieces clattered to the floor, the sound echoing through the church. "Clifford, wedge that crowbar between the wall and the door." He pointed.

Clifford obliged.

"When I give the signal, pull the door *into* the church." He gestured toward the altar. "Make sure the door doesn't fall on poor Lieutenant Somersby." He raised the sledgehammer over his head. "You know I'm doing this for you, ma chérie. Not for him." He brought it down hard and shouted, "Now, old man."

His back against the wall for leverage, Clifford cranked on the crowbar. The veins in his neck bulged as he pressed against the bar. The door lumbered forward and then crashed to the floor. Clifford jumped out of the way just in time.

"Get him on the stretcher." I rushed to Archie's side. Crumpled in a heap, covered in blood, he lay unconscious. *Please, oh, please. Let him live.* I repeated my silent prayer. Of course, I'd seen gunshot wounds before. And I'd seen men die—even men I'd cared about. But I'd never seen my entire future bleeding out before my eyes. He needed to go to hospital. But where? We couldn't take Archie to a state-run hospital. He had attacked the

Kremlin, after all. But if we didn't get him to a hospital right away, he would most certainly die. Fredricks and Clifford lifted him onto the stretcher. Archie moaned.

"He's still alive." I reached for his hand. He was holding fast to a piece of paper, a ripped photograph. It was covered in blood. He wouldn't let go of it. He was holding onto it for dear life. It must have been important. He wouldn't let me take it from his hand.

The men carried him out to the lorry. Fredricks had parked it in an alley behind the church. We couldn't risk the police seeing us carrying a badly wounded British agent. Kitty opened the canvas flap at the back of the lorry and the men slid the stretcher inside.

"Burn." Archie was trembling from the cold. "Punch... Fiona." Clearly, he was delirious from loss of blood. "Fiona." He passed out again. What did he mean? I didn't blame him if he did want to punch me.

"Here." Fredricks sloughed off his heavy wool coat and handed it to me. "He's in shock. You need to keep him warm."

I took the coat. "Thank you." He might be an enemy spy, but Fredricks had a good heart, whatever Archie and Kitty said about him.

"Goodbye, ma chérie." There was a note of sadness in his voice. "I wish you nothing but happiness." Fredricks bowed slightly.

"Aren't you coming with us?" I put my hand on his sleeve.

He stared down at my hand and I pulled it away. "We both know that's not a good idea. Your lieutenant would just as soon kill me as look at me." He smiled. "And there's only room in your heart for one of us." He reached out, took my hand, and kissed it. "*Au revoir*, ma chérie."

I watched as he rounded the corner and then disappeared.

"Let's go," Kitty called out from the front of the lorry.

"Where?" I climbed in the back and covered Archie with Fredricks's coat. All of the main hospitals were run by the Bolsheviks.

"To Cheka headquarters." Kitty opened the passenger door and Poppy jumped inside.

"Good lord." Clifford stood by the driver's door. "The police?"

"Olga will know where to take him." Kitty climbed in and slammed the door. "Let's go."

"Righto." Clifford took the driver's seat. "Ready, old bean?" he called out.

"Ready." I sat on a bench in the back of the lorry. Archie's face was pale and ghostly. I felt his wrist. His pulse was weak. I took out a handkerchief and pressed it to his wound. He was still clutching that blood-stained photograph.

The lorry jolted to life and then rolled forward. I held onto the lorry's metal frame with one hand and pressed my hanky against Archie's side with the other. Within minutes, the white fabric was blood red and soaked through. I ripped another piece off my skirt. By the time the lorry came to a stop, my hands were wet with blood.

Time seemed to be moving in slow motion. The exhaust from the idling lorry penetrated the canvas. Acrid and burning, it assaulted my lungs. The motor growled, making the bench vibrate. I could see my breath in the frigid air. I stared down at Archie. Was he still breathing? I put my ear to his mouth. The warmth of his breath was ever so slight. I laid my hand on his chest to confirm. Thank goodness. He hadn't died yet. But he would if we didn't hurry and get him to a hospital. What was taking so long? What if the Cheka came out to investigate? I hoped to heaven Kitty knew what she was doing.

Exhausted, I put my head in my hands and stared down at the blood-splattered floor of the lorry. There it was. The torn photograph. Archie must have dropped it. I picked it up and held it into the light streaming in through the back flap. Good heavens. I gave a little gasp. It was a black-and-white photograph of me in front of the Metropol Hotel.

KITTY'S INTERLUDE
10 MARCH, 5.30 P.M.

Kitty had shed the Petrov Special Cleaners costume and was back in her normal clothes. Normal clothes for spy work. Or at least the public-facing side of her persona. A fuchsia gabardine frock with a white fur collar, a tailored peach wool coat, white gloves, and button-up black boots. As she stepped out of the lorry, she quickly tucked stray hairs into her makeshift chignon, and scooped Poppy off the passenger seat. She couldn't forget her most important prop. The adorable Pekingese.

Cheka headquarters was buzzing with officers, some wearing uniforms, but most wearing street clothes. It was difficult to tell the perps from the coppers. A dozen or so men and women were lined up against one wall, all looking miserable. One man lit up a cigarette and immediately a copper whacked it out of his hand onto the floor. "No cigarettes for prisoners," he barked.

Kitty went to the front desk. Petting Poppy, she asked to see Mrs. Motya Pasternak, head of records, Olga's cover. Kitty's Russian was flawless, with a Moscow accent that signaled cultured but not aristocratic. She peppered her conversation with just the right balance of giggles to words to disarm her interlocutor. Poppy wagged her tail and made doe eyes at the receptionist, a gangly woman with an overbite. The woman couldn't resist. Who could? The receptionist laughed and reached out to pat Poppy's head. Worked like a charm. A few minutes later, Kitty was escorted to Mrs. Pasternak's office.

Olga's eyes went wide. Obviously, she wasn't comfortable with Kitty visiting police headquarters. Glancing over her shoulder to make sure the receptionist was gone, Kitty approached the desk. She stood next to her friend. "Archie is bleeding out," she whispered. "We need a hospital." In a normal voice, she said, "Your mother has taken a turn and wanted me to fetch you."

Poppy whimpered.

Olga closed a file folder and stood up. "My mother." Her voice was full of concern. "What happened?" A file in hand, she turned to face a filing cabinet. "Take him to Yuri Botkin, the tsar's doctor's son." Olga's lips didn't move as she whispered, "He and his sister run an underground clinic off the Garden Ring, just across Krymsky Bridge." She tore a small corner from one of the sheets in the folder. Taking a pencil from behind her ear, she jotted down an address and tucked it into Kitty's coat pocket. "Tell my mother I will come as soon as possible."

Kitty palmed the address and made for the door.

"Thank you, comrade." Olga gave her a knowing look. "Peace, land, bread."

"Peace, land, bread." Kitty nodded. At a steady pace, she walked back down the hall and out of the police station.

Once outside, she quickened her pace. "I've got it," she said as she opened the passenger door. Poppy jumped onto the seat. She removed the corner of paper from her pocket and climbed into the lorry. "Twenty-three Zubovsky Boulevard," she read aloud. "Step on it."

16

THE CLINIC

The underground clinic wasn't literally underground. But it was where tsarists and anti-Bolshevik warriors took their wounded. Overcrowded but clean, the clinic was in a large garage off a back alley behind a compound of some sort. The sign over the entrance read *Tsvety*. If I wasn't mistaken, that meant "Flowers." As you first walked in, there was a long narrow trough filled with empty milk bottles. Some of them had bedraggled flowers poking out their tops.

I paced the hallway, waiting for word of Archie. The doctor had taken him into surgery an hour ago. Why was it taking so long? No news was probably good news. If he'd died, someone would have told me. Wouldn't they? Then again, Yuri Botkin and his staff were run ragged. But what doctors and nurses weren't these days? I applauded anyone who wanted to help his fellows, tsarist, Bolshevik, or otherwise. Sickness and death didn't care about ideology. Although I doubted that the state-run hospitals were in back alleys operating as florist shops.

Kitty and Clifford had gone to get something to eat. How

could they think of food when Archie might die on the operating table?

"Excuse me, Miss Figg?" With the heavy Russian accent, Figg sounded like Feek. It was Dr. Botkin. I held my breath.

"Your fiancé is in recovery." He pointed down the hall. "We have him sedated and he probably won't regain consciousness for many hours." His delicate hands danced as he talked. "But you may sit with him if you like."

My fiancé. "Thank you, doctor." My heart sang. Archie was alive.

"He is very weak. But if he makes it through the night, he has a good chance to survive."

I blinked. He wasn't out of the woods yet. He had to make it through the night. In that case, I wasn't leaving. "I'll sit with him."

The doctor nodded. "Follow me." He escorted me to a room at the end of the hall. Rows of cots lined both sides of the room. All the cots were occupied. The doctor led me to Archie's cot. Next to it was a small wooden chair and a nightstand. A cup of water sat upon the stand. "You may sit with him for as long as you like."

"Thank you." I sat down and watched as the doctor left the room. When he was gone, I stared at the floor. Finally, I forced myself to look at Archie. He had aged a decade overnight. His once lovely face was gaunt and had a sickly yellow tinge. His body looked shrunken under the gray blanket. Even the curl of hair that usually fell across his forehead had flattened out and stuck to his temple. I slumped in the chair and gazed at him. *If he makes it through the night.* I went back to my silent prayers and bargains with God.

I must have dozed off. Kitty's hand on my shoulder woke me. "Aunt Fiona," she whispered. "You go get some proper sleep and a meal. I'll stay with him."

I shook my head. "I won't leave him. Not tonight." Not ever.

"Are you sure?" Her voice was soft as she took my hand. "You need to take care of yourself, too."

"I'm sure." I squeezed her hand. "I want to be here when he wakes up."

She pulled a package of biscuits from her pocket. "At least eat something."

I gave her a weak smile and took the packet. "Thanks, love."

She took a few steps and then stopped and looked back at me, like there was something more she wanted to say. Instead, she shook her head and then headed for the door.

To block out the moans and sorrows of the wounded men, I concentrated on Archie. On his face. His hair. His nose. His eyelashes. I willed him to recover. Laying my hand on top of the blanket where his hand was underneath, I focused on sending my life force into him. Could I transfer my energy to his body? I closed my eyes and tried to feel the connection between us. A lightness pricked at my palm. A tingling sensation. The expansion of breath.

I don't know how much time had passed. My back ached and my head was throbbing. But I didn't remove my hand from Archie's. "You're going to mend," I whispered. "You're going to be alright."

A cramp in my leg made me wince and remove my hand. I rubbed my calf with numb fingers and reminded myself that my discomfort was nothing compared to the suffering of these soldiers.

"Fiona?" His voice was but a thin thread.

"Yes, darling." I forced a smile.

"Thirsty." His eyes were dull and hard.

I picked up the glass of water from the nightstand and held it to his cracked lips. He drank greedily, like a man who'd crossed a great desert. It seemed harsh, even cruel, to withdraw the glass. But he was drinking too fast. "Slowly," I whispered.

He extended a bruised hand out from under the cover. Trembling, he reached for the glass. I spoke softly and playfully but with a firmness, as if I was speaking to a child. After I gave him another drink, he settled back into a more restful sleep. As his body relaxed, so did mine.

The next thing I knew, Kitty was back. She tugged at my sleeve. "Aunt Fiona." She bent down so her face was just inches from mine. "Wake up."

I stared at her. My mouth was dry, and my tongue felt swollen. Like the time in Vienna after I'd drunk too many gin fizzes.

"You've got to get out of here." Kitty knelt in front of me. "The Cheka are looking for you." She held up a wanted poster with my picture on it. "These are everywhere. Someone will recognize you and turn you in."

"Why?" My sleepy mind was like cotton wool.

"For the murder of Iron Victor." She took me by the elbow and stood me up. "You've got to go." Tugging at my jacket, she forced me to move.

I glanced back at Archie. His cheeks had regained some color and his chest moved up and down in the regular rhythm of deep slumber.

"I'll stay with him." Kitty pushed me now. "Clifford is waiting with the lorry. He'll take you back to the consulate. The Cheka know better than to bother you there. Even they don't want an international incident with Great Britain."

"You'll stay with him?" I gritted my teeth. I didn't want to leave. "Tell him... tell him that I..."

"I will." She nodded. "Now go before it's too late."

My head down, I hurried out of the room, back down the hall, and out of the clinic. Its motor running, the lorry was waiting in front. I went to the passenger side window. Shielding my eyes with my hand, I pressed my face against the glass and peered in. With his pipe clamped between his teeth, Clifford gestured for me to get in. I opened the door and hopped up onto the seat.

"Good to see you, old thing." His smile was reassuring.

"Likewise." Tears welled in my eyes. I wanted to throw my arms around him and cry my eyes out. To stop myself, I bit my lip until I tasted blood. Poppy wagged her tail and licked my face. I pulled her into a tight embrace. "Thank you, Poppy-poo."

Poppy curled up on my lap. We rode in silence through the sleepy streets of Moscow as they welcomed dawn's downy light. A somber gauzy violet. Not the single-minded intensity of the mad tuba. But the diffuse and muffled sound of a memory. A memory of hope.

* * *

Once I was tucked safely back in the consulate, I took a quick bath and changed my clothes. When I folded my dirty skirt, I discovered the blood-stained photograph that Archie had clutched for dear life. The photograph of me, taken days ago in front of the Metropol Hotel. Was Archie spying on me? How did he get that photograph? Who had taken it and why? Did Archie know I'd come to Moscow to meet Fredricks? That I wasn't really on assignment? That I came for a romantic tryst? Cringing, I tucked it into my handbag and then joined Clifford in the other room.

While Clifford enjoyed a smoke, I put on the kettle. Poppy followed me into the kitchen and kept a watchful eye on me. I needed sleep. But I was too exhausted... and too vulnerable. With the ambassadors gone, the flat vibrated at a different register. The subterranean hum of the heating system and the sound of distant sirens. Why? Russia had surrendered. For them, the war was over. Would it ever be over for us? Not if it meant giving in to the Germans.

I made two cups of tea and brought them out to the table. Poppy's nails clicked on the hard floor as she trotted after me. His pipe still firmly in place, Clifford smiled up at me as I sat the cup in front of him. "Thanks, old bean."

I sat down across from him and blew on my tea. Now what? Was I to be a prisoner in the consulate? How would I get back to London? I was a wanted woman. The only way out was to clear my name. I had to find Iron Victor's killer. Only when I could present him on a platter for the Cheka would I be free. If I had the proper paperwork to leave the country disguised as a man, I could make my escape. But without papers, there was no way I'd make it out of Russia. There were Cheka at every border. Clearing my name was the only way out.

"So, who do you think is the mole?" Clifford asked out of the blue.

The mole. I'd forgotten about the mole. "Sir Robert Lockhart is in jail. Chances are, he didn't betray the plan." And Archie had been severely wounded. His name was clear. What a relief. He wasn't the mole. That left the Russian revolutionary Boris Savinkov and the Ace of Spies, Sidney Reilly. Savinkov had been the get-away driver. He got away alright. And so did Reilly. Neither Kitty nor Clifford had seen hide nor hair of them since the botched kidnapping attempt. "Who had the most to gain?"

"I never did trust the Russian bloke." Clifford leaned back in his chair. "And something about that Reilly set my teeth on edge."

"Maybe they were in it together?" I sipped my tea.

"But why?" Clifford asked. "Why betray the plan?"

"Money or ideology." I slipped my notebook out of my skirt pocket. "Either they were bribed, or they were secretly Bolshevik loyalists." I wrote their names at the top of one page. "I'd say we wait and see which one turns up. If neither of them does, then they were in cahoots."

"And what are we going to do about you, old girl?" Clifford took a small flask out of his waistcoat pocket and poured a bit of amber liquid into his tea. "Fancy a pick-me-up?" He held out the flask.

A knock-me-down, more like. I shook my head. "We have to find Iron Victor's killer and clear my name."

"How?" He sipped his spiked tea. "I say." His eyes sparkled. "Since you can't go out, I can investigate while you watch Poppy." He reached down and scooped up the pup, who was sitting near his chair gazing up at him.

I tightened my lips. That was hardly the plan I had in mind. Not a chance I would leave my fate in his bumbling hands. Not that I didn't trust him, mind you. "First, I'm going to make a list of suspects and clues." I flipped to a clean page in my notebook.

"Good idea." He puffed. "Who else was in the house?"

"His wife, Mrs. Volodarsky." I put her name at the bottom of the page. "Spouses are always prime suspects when it came to murder." What wife hadn't wanted to murder her husband at some time or other? "Iron Victor had visitors the night he died. Nocturnal visitors." I didn't bother to mention that one of them was Fredricks. But I put his name at the top of my list, none-theless. If I hadn't been preoccupied with Archie, I could have properly interviewed Fredricks. If he had murdered Iron Victor, that would certainly explain why he had to go into hiding and why the Bolsheviks wouldn't be happy with him. But what was his motive? Was Iron Victor a double agent? Fredricks loved to target German agents who'd turned. Not likely Victor was working for the British given his opinions on our literature and culture. Then again, perhaps he was putting on an act. If so, he was jolly convincing.

"Who?" Clifford drained his cup. "And why at night?"

"Precisely." I tapped my pad with my pencil. "Countess Natalia came to beg for her husband's release." I put her name on my list. Could she have killed Iron Victor?

"You don't think a countess committed murder?" He looked incredulous. Of course, he never imagined a woman, especially a lovely aristocrat, could do something so heinous.

"A woman is as capable of murder as a man." Would she murder him out of vengeance? Yet I'd heard her leave with Fredricks. And Victor was still alive, speaking to the second man. "There was another man."

"Who?" Clifford pulled out the flask again and poured more whiskey into his cup.

"If we knew that, we'd likely have our killer." Who was the second man? I wrote "Mystery Man" and circled it twice.

"Is he the mole?" He sipped his drink.

"If the mole killed Victor, then it must have been either Savinkov or Reilly." Clifford finished his whiskey and went back to his pipe.

"But why tell him about the plan and then kill him? It doesn't make sense."

"I suppose you're right, old girl." He shrugged.

The only clue I had to go on was that open compartment behind the painting. I needed to get back to the house and find out what was taken from that safe. Oh, and those cigar butts. They were still tucked away in the pocket of my other skirt. And as soon as Kitty got back from the clinic, I'd have her examine them. She might see something I'd missed.

"I have to get back into Iron Victor's house." There must be more evidence in that library. I hadn't had enough time to inspect it properly before Mrs. V found me in the room with her husband's dead body.

"And just how will you do that?" Clifford chuckled.

"I have my ways." I had the perfect disguise. A new one I'd purchased at Angel's Fancy Dress Shop before I'd left London. And a new beard, too. The most impressive beard of my collection. I got butterflies just thinking about it.

KITTY'S INTERLUDE
11 MARCH, 7 A.M.

Kitty tried to sit still. She really did. Fidgeting in the chair next to Archie's cot, she regretted promising Aunt Fiona she'd stay with him. The only thing she hated worse than doing nothing was being in a hospital. She could deliver a butterfly kick to the head or cut a man's throat, but she never could stand the sight of sickness. When she was ten, she'd lost her mother and her youngest sister to tuberculosis. They were living on the streets and by their wits. She and her two younger sisters picked pockets, while her mother did favors for strange men. She'd tended their sick beds. But they died anyway.

In her head, she rehearsed the foot-fighting technique she'd learned in France. Whenever she got bored or sad, she distracted herself by imagining her moves in a fighting match. She and her instructor, Marie Marvingt, used to have brilliant matches. But none of the other girls could come close to Kitty's skill. She wished her stupid cover gave her more time and space to practice.

The bundle of blankets next to her stirred. She looked down at Archie. He was messed up. Good thing Aunt Fiona insisted they look for him. He would have died otherwise. Now maybe he and Fiona would patch things up and get married. Archie wasn't the brightest star in the sky, but he was a good man. And honest. Unless you counted his work, of course. Aunt Fiona could do worse. Much worse. She thought of Fredrick Fredricks. Anything to get him out of the picture.

"Fiona?" Archie croaked like a frog. "Are you here?"

"No." She sighed. "It's me, Kitty."

"Oh." Deflated, he seemed to sink deeper into the cot.

"Don't sound so disappointed." She picked at one of her fingernails. "If it weren't for Fiona, I wouldn't be here."

"Thanks." He finally opened his eyes. Bloodshot eyes. The red in the whites made the green of the irises glow. "Where's Fiona?"

"She's a wanted woman." Kitty smirked. "Haven't you heard?" She pulled the wanted poster from her coat pocket and held it up. "The Cheka are looking for her for Victor's murder."

"Holy hell." Archie sat up on his elbows. "Is she alright?"

"Yeah." She smiled. "Knowing her, using her little notebook and list of suspects, she's homing in on the real killer by now."

Archie grimaced.

"Are you alright?" She handed him the glass of water from the nightstand. "Here, drink. You look terrible."

"I'm not thirsty." With effort, he slid up and leaned against the wall. "Fiona didn't kill Iron Victor."

"I know that, and you know that." Kitty shook her head. "If you'd marry her, maybe she'd stay out of trouble."

"Hey. If I had my way, we'd be hitched already." He ran a hand through his hair.

"Yeah. And have a kid on the way." She laughed. Imagine Aunt Fiona as a mother!

"You know her as well as anyone." His tone was serious. "She's a brick and I adore her. And I think she likes me, too." He stared down at his hands and picked at a thread on the blanket. "So why won't she marry me?"

Kitty shrugged. "She's afraid, I guess."

"Afraid of me?" His voice cracked.

"Afraid of *losing* you." She resisted adding, *you dummy*. "She lost one husband already. He cheated on her. So why should she trust another man? And then he went and got himself killed. Gone forever." She leveled her gaze at those bloodshot eyes. "No wonder she's afraid."

17

RETURNING TO THE SCENE

I was afraid. My hand trembled as I rang the bell. What if someone recognized me? I patted my mustache and beard, which was a great bushy number streaked with gray and a good ten inches long. My brows were two caterpillars attached with spirit glue. My hair—or should I say wig—was parted down the middle and slick with Macassar oil. I wore round wire spectacles. The glass was thick but clear. My suit had fine brocade and silk buttons complete with a gold pocket watch in the manner of Sir Edward Burnett Tylor, the famous professor and keeper of the Oxford library museum. In fact, it was his persona I'd borrowed. I'd even had cards made. The man had died a year ago. Hopefully that news hadn't yet reached Moscow. Disguised as an Oxford don and rare-book purveyor, I hoped to gain access to Iron Victor's library and re-examine the scene of the crime. And Kitty's forensics case passed as a book examination kit.

I held the leather case in one hand and shifted from foot to foot as I waited for someone to come to the door. The afternoon sun warmed my back. Which was a relief, since the brisk breeze was burning my eyeballs. Finally, a young woman I recognized as the parlor maid answered the door. In broken Russian, I tried to explain I was there about the rare books in Mr. Volodarsky's library. Mrs. Volodarsky had commissioned me to assess their value.

The maid in turn explained that the mistress of the house was out at the moment, which of course I already knew. In fact, that was the point. I was counting on Mrs. V being at her Monday bridge game. From what I'd seen, even bereavement couldn't come between her and her weekly bridge game. I continued in English, insisting I see the books as soon as possible. I was due to catch an evening train. I handed her my card and reiterated the urgency of my visit, this time in Russian. Very poor Russian. But what I lacked in proficiency, I made up for in passion. Spitting words like nails eventually worked. Wiping her face with the corner of her apron, the young woman gave in and led me to the library.

For a few minutes, she stood in the doorway watching me. I sat my case on the floor and pretended to examine a book, very slowly, lingering over the bindings and studying each page. The maid must have got bored. Finally, she shut the library door and left me to it. As soon as she did, I scurried to where the Kandinsky painting hung. It was reattached to the wall. I wanted to re-examine the contents of the safe. There must be a clue there. It wasn't just a coincidence that it was left open the night Iron Victor was killed. There had to be a connection between the open safe and the dead man.

I lightly ran a finger across the bottom of the frame. There must be some way to move the painting and reveal the safe. A lever or a button. I ran my hand across the mantel. And then up the side of the frame. Aha. A small button met my finger. I pressed it and the painting released with a click. I gently swung it open. Blast. How would I open the safe? My lockpick set was useless. And my crash course in espionage didn't include safe cracking. I would have to come back to the safe. For now, I'd better survey the rest of the room before Mrs. V returned from playing bridge.

The maids had cleaned the room since that fateful night. But some clues remained. The file folder still sat on the edge of the desk. The whiskey decanter was in the middle of the coffee table. The glasses were gone, unfortunately. The ashtray had been emptied. Luckily, I'd snagged those two cigar butts. I hoped Kitty got my letter. Back at the consulate, I'd left an envelope containing the cigar butts and a note asking her to test them for toxins or anything that could kill a man.

I glanced around to make sure no one was watching and then laid the case on the coffee table and unlocked it. Opening it was almost as exciting as opening my mustache case. Inside, Kitty had small brown collection envelopes and test tubes. The tiny envelopes were tucked in a special pocket. The test tubes each had their own individual band holding them in place. On the inside of the top of the case, various tools also had their own pockets, including long tweezers, a putty knife, and a brush for dusting fingerprints. The bottom of the case had slots for jars of powders and testing solutions. I'd leave those to Kitty, who would probably be furious when she discovered I'd taken her case.

I dropped to my hands and knees in front of the divan. Crawling around on the Persian rug, I looked under the furniture for clues. Surely one of Iron Victor's visitors had left something. The principle of exchange. They'd left something and taken something. I just had to determine what. I withdrew a magnifying glass from my waistcoat and examined the carpet fibers where the body had been found. A patch of dried whitish powder caught my eye. I'd come prepared. Along with the putty knife, I slid a tiny envelope from its pouch. I scraped a bit of the white powder into the envelope, sealed it, and put it into another pouch in the case. Kitty could analyze it later.

With my cheek to the floor, I peered under the sofa. Aha. Along with one of Luka's building blocks, there was an extra whiskey glass. Anna was telling the truth. There was a fifth visitor that night. With my pencil, I dragged it out from under the sofa and held it up. Probably Iron Victor's. He'd dropped it when he keeled over, and it rolled under the sofa.

And what's this? One small cuff-link. Perhaps there had been a struggle and somehow, I hadn't heard it. I dropped the cuff-link into the glass and then wrapped the glass in felt and tucked it into the pouch with my carpet sample. After I'd conducted a thorough search of the carpet and underneath the furniture, steadying myself against Victor's high-backed chair, I stood up. What next?

I went to the desk and picked up the file folder. The one the men had been discussing when they mentioned my name and Maria Bochkareva, aka Happy. When I opened it, I was met with a ripped black-and-white photograph of the Metropol Hotel stapled to some papers. The person was torn out of the photograph, only her hat remained. A cloche hat. I held the photograph closer. Good heavens. It was my cloche hat. How on earth did they get that photo? Had the Cheka been spying on me from the moment I arrived in Moscow? My stomach sank. This wasn't just any photograph. It was the other half of the picture Archie clutched in the lorry. How did Archie come by that photograph? Had the mole taken it and then lost it in the chaos at the Kremlin? And Archie picked it up? Why would the mole have a picture of me? And what was it doing in this file? More importantly, what was half of it doing in Archie's hand?

Blimey. I had a dreadful thought. Surely Iron Victor recognized me from the photograph. Before he died, he must have known I was a British spy. A knot in my chest felt like someone had reached in and grabbed my heart. If it hadn't been for the killer, I'd probably be dead by now. Hauled in front of a firing squad and shot. I shuddered. If the last nanny was shot for playing chess, imagine what Victor would have done if he'd found a spy in his house.

More to the point, who had ripped me out of the photograph and why?

I put the file back exactly the way it was and then continued my search. Walking the circumference of the room, I took note of every piece of furniture, every bookcase, every knick-knack. There must be some evidence as to the identity of the mystery man. I stopped in front of the phonograph cabinet. What would they think of next? The large mahogany cabinet was waist-high. A crank protruded from one side. Brass knobs on two front door panels invited opening. Carefully, I opened them. A neat stack of phonograph records met my gaze. I'd never seen a phonograph outside of this house. Should I get one for my flat? I shook my head. Probably couldn't afford it. Must cost a fortune. I lifted the lid. Inside, the heavy brass arm rested on a stand. A phonograph record sat atop a green felt cloth attached to a metal disc. Was this what Iron Victor was listening to the night he died?

I expected to see his favorite, Stravinsky's "The Fox," the music he'd been playing before he was killed. Instead, if I wasn't mistaken, the label on the phonograph record read *V. Lenin's Speeches 1917*. A recording of Lenin's speeches. Had Mrs. V been here listening to Lenin's speeches after her husband died? I lifted the vinyl disc and took a closer look. Did I dare listen to the recording? I put the phonograph record back atop the green felt pad. I lifted the brass arm. It was thick and heavy and cool to the touch. What if I put it on and it blasted sound throughout the house? Someone would come running and I'd have to explain myself. I had another idea. I picked up the phonograph recording again and then closed the lid. I wrapped the phonograph record in felt cloth and laid it inside Kitty's forensics case. It just fit. Now if I could transport it without breaking it... and find someone with a phonograph. Did I know any wealthy Russians?

I glanced at my watch. Mrs. V would be back from her bridge game soon. My last challenge was the safe. I went back to the Kandinsky painting and then stood staring at it. I turned the dial. What numbers might Iron Victor use as a combination? I had no bloody idea.

"I haven't seen you here before." The small Russian voice came from behind me. "What are you doing in my papa's library?"

My hand flew to my chest. I whirled around to face my accuser. "Anna."

The girl gave me a quizzical look. "Miss Figg, you came back!" Darting around the sofa and then the chair, she made a game of running over to me. When she reached me, she threw her arms around me. "You came back!"

"How did you know it was me?" I held her at arm's length.

She looked up at me with a mischievous grin. "No one else says Anna the way you do."

Golly. Was I that obvious? I thought I'd done a brilliant job on my disguise. But I couldn't fool Anna. She was a clever little mite. Standing at my side, she pointed up at the safe. "I know the combination."

My bushy eyebrows arched in surprise. "You do?"

"It's my birthday." She puffed out her chest. "Eleven, six, nineteen, seven." She counted them on her fingers. "Four numbers."

"June eleventh, nineteen hundred and seven." I smiled. "Only three months from now."

She gave an exaggerated nod. "Papa promised to take me to

see the Bolshoi Ballet for my birthday." Her smile faded. "Now he's gone."

I felt for her. I really did. He was a tyrant, but he was her father. "I'm sorry." I stroked her cheek.

"Aren't you going to open it?" Her countenance brightened. "You are a spy, aren't you?"

"Good heavens." My eyes went wide. "Whatever gave you that idea?"

"Mama said that's why you left." She shrugged. "I don't mind. My favorite stories are the ones with spies. I didn't know girls could be spies."

"Of course girls can be spies." I straightened to my full height. "Very good ones."

"I want to be a spy, too." She smiled. "Just like you."

Blimey. I'd never had anyone look up to me before. Is this what it would be like to have a daughter? I'd never know. *Sigh*.

"Go ahead." She pointed. "Open it."

"Yes, ma'am." I followed her instructions as she told me which way to turn the dial. When the safe clicked open, she clapped her hands together.

"Papa forbade me from opening it." The mischievous gleam came back to her pretty eyes. "But I did anyway."

"I bet you did." Were daughters always as disobedient and precocious as Anna? A dangerous combination.

"Want to know how?" She beamed. "I dragged that chair from the desk. After Mama and Papa went to bed. When I was sleep-walking."

"Sleepwalking?" I tilted my head. "Really."

"You'll never guess what I found in there." She started counting on her fingers again. "Royal princess jewelry, stacks of money, and a gun."

Exactly what I'd seen after Victor was killed. Royal jewelry and stacks of money could be motives for murder. But in that case, why didn't the killer take them? Had he been interrupted by Victor, killed him, and then lost his nerve and left? I shook my head. If it was a robbery, then why didn't I hear a fight? And why weren't there signs of a struggle? Victor wouldn't have sat by and watched while a thief rummaged through his safe. Unless he was forced to at gunpoint. Surely I would have heard something.

I looked inside the safe. It was empty. Had Mrs. V emptied it after the murder? I knew the jewelry, money, and gun were here. Could the thief/murderer have been hiding in the library and took off with the loot after everyone cleared out? I glanced around. Aside from my hiding place under the desk, I didn't see any obvious hiding place.

I reached inside and felt around the dark corners to make sure I didn't miss anything. My fingertip brushed against a bit of paper. I plucked it out of the safe and examined it. It appeared to be the top corner of an official brief embossed with the same seal I'd seen on the stationery in Victor's desk and on Fredricks's note at the hotel. There were only two words in Russian. And it was stamped "OB." The same notation I'd seen on the White Rose Directive file. "What does OB stand for?" I held out the paper fragment to Anna.

"OB." She peered at it. "Top-secret." She looked up at me. "It says Ambassador Plot."

"Ambassador Plot." Now I knew what the thief was after. A top-secret file on Operation Ambassadors. Did the killer steal the file and dispose of Victor because he knew about the plot? But I'd heard the mystery man *tell* Victor about the Ambassador Plot. Why would he tell Victor and then kill him and steal the file? It made no sense.

The killer must have been the other mystery person.

The fifth whiskey glass. The fifth visitor.

KITTY'S INTERLUDE
11 MARCH, NOON

Kitty opened the envelope and dumped the contents onto the table. Two cigar butts and a note.

Kitty, dear. Please test these for toxins strong enough to kill a man instantly.

She crumpled up the note and lobbed it across the room and into the bin. Poppy chased after it, tipped the bin over, retrieved the note, and brought it back. "If Aunt Fiona wanted me to test these..." she poked at the butts, "she shouldn't have taken my forensics case." Kitty took the wad of paper from the dog's mouth. "Right, Poppy-poo?" Poppy barked in agreement.

18

THE CHEKA

From Iron Victor's house, I hopped on the nearest bus and headed back into the heart of the city. The consolation of a long bus ride was taking in the scenery. Moscow was a glorious city, but it had seen better days. Everyone wished the war would end. Probably none more so than the Muscovites. Unfortunately, their exit from the Great War only gave the civil war more ammunition.

My stomach growled as I stepped off the bus in front of the Metropol Hotel. I shook off a chill and headed straight for suite 315. I didn't expect Fredricks to be there. But I hoped his decoy could inform the cad that I needed a meeting right away. I suspected Fredricks knew more about Iron Victor's assassination than anyone. And he'd better spill the beans. Or I'd be going to jail.

I knocked at suite 315. Nothing. I knocked again. Silence. I put my ear to the door. "Duke, are you in there?" I could swear I heard someone stirring inside. I leaned closer and again pressed my ear to the door. Suddenly, it opened, and I fell forward. Fredricks caught me in his arms. His bare arms.

He was naked from the waist up and wearing only a pair of trousers. His feet were bare. Curls of wet hair dripped along the ridge of his shoulders. I looked up into his eyes.

"Ma chérie." He laughed. "Why are you wearing that ghastly beard?"

Golly. I'd completely forgotten I was wandering around as Sir Edward Burnett Tylor. I dropped Kitty's forensics case.

"You look like a bearded tamarin," he said into my hair—or should I say wig. The smell of his sandalwood soap made me giddy.

I released myself from his arms and patted my beard. "Bearded tamarin, eh? I won't ask."

"An adorable little Peruvian monkey with a great mustache." He swallowed a chuckle. "I'd love to show you around Peru someday." He tilted his head and got the most mischievous look in his eyes. "That is, when you finally decide to throw over your young lieutenant." He put his hand on my sleeve. "He did live, didn't he?" he asked with exaggerated concern.

I swatted his hand away.

Feigning injury, he pulled his hand away. "You could thank me."

"Thank you." I had to admit, if he hadn't arrived with the lorry when he did, Archie would have bled to death. I shuddered to think.

"I suppose I wasn't acting in my own best interests." He brushed imaginary lint from my sleeve. "But as long as you're happy."

"Quit saying that." I leveled my gaze. "You're the last person to believe we're put on earth for happiness."

"A pig satisfied and all that rot." He waved his hand in front of his face as if shooing a fly.

"I have no idea what you're talking about." *Sigh*. Sometimes he tried my patience.

"Your own John Stuart Mill." He gave me a questioning look.

I shrugged.

"I'd rather be Socrates unhappy than a pig satisfied." He raised his eyebrow. "No?"

"No." A pig satisfied, my flat foot.

"You'd better come in, ma chérie, before the Cheka arrive and catch us both." He picked up my case and gestured me in. "May I take your hat?"

I handed him my fedora.

"Speaking of the Cheka," I said as I marched into the suite, "you need to tell me everything you know about Iron Victor's murder."

"What makes you think I know anything?" He shut the door behind me. "Your coat?" He held out his hand.

I shed my coat and held it out to him. "You always know everything."

He sat the forensics case behind the door. "You flatter me." He smiled and hung my coat and hat on a hook. "But like Socrates, I only know that I don't know."

Exasperating man. "If you don't tell me who killed Iron Victor, the Cheka will pin it on me, and I'll be executed." Saying it out loud gave me a chill.

"Sit down, ma chérie." He took my hand and led me to the sitting area near the fireplace. Although I'd been in the space before, it looked smaller with Fredricks in it. Even the draft coming through the broken window seemed less severe.

"You look pallid. Are you quite alright?" He was still holding my hand.

I yanked it away. "No, I'm not alright." My head gave an involuntary jerk. "I'm wanted for murder. Archie is fighting for his life. And you... you..."

"You need a brandy." He went to the sideboard and returned with two small glasses of brandy. "To us." He held up his glass.

"There is no *us*." I refused to toast. I'd humiliated myself by following him to this godforsaken place and he'd abandoned me. "Can't you be serious for once?" I slumped into the chair. "I'm really not in the mood for your cheek."

"What are you in the mood for?" He sat across from me, smiling like the cat who got the canary. A very attractive half-naked cat.

I tightened my lips. I had nothing to go on. If Fredricks wouldn't help me, I'd surely be shot. I stared down at my brogues, wondering how I'd managed to get myself into this mess. "Please just tell me what you know about Iron Victor's murder."

"Victor was alive the last time I saw him, as you well know." He sipped his brandy.

"What do you mean by that?" I gazed down into the amber liquid filling my glass. I didn't dare look at him. Every time I did, the tingling across the surface of my body made me forget why I came.

"You were there." He grinned. "I smelled your sweet perfume and sensed your lovely presence."

"Right." Sweet perfume, my bushy beard. I gave him a dirty look. Or at least I tried to... My cheeks burned and no doubt had turned a rosy red.

He sighed. "I knew you'd been assigned to go undercover as the governess, and I figured you wouldn't let Victor out of your sight." He crossed one long leg over the other. "You must know who killed him. You couldn't have left the library before the killer did."

"If you must know..." I took a sip. The alcohol burned all the way down. "I was hiding under the desk and didn't see a thing." I didn't tell him I'd fallen asleep on the job.

"I suspected as much." He chuckled. "I had to resist the urge to crawl under there with you."

Imagine... no, don't imagine. "Don't be impertinent." I brushed my trousers. "Tell me what you know." I leveled my gaze. "My life depends on it." My attempt to look intimidating didn't last. Sitting there with his tanned torso and long black hair, looking every bit a Greek god, it was obvious why one of his nicknames was Apollo.

"I don't know who killed Victor." He drained his glass. "But I do know it will set in motion the White Rose Directive." He went to the closet and withdrew a blousy white shirt.

"WRD," I said under my breath.

"In retaliation for the assassination of the chief of police," he pulled the shirt over his head, "the Cheka plans to kill the tsar and his family." He fetched his socks and boots and returned to his chair. "Without the tsar, there can be no tsarist." He pulled on a boot. As he finished dressing, he told me how the Bolsheviks planned to move the royal family into even further isolation and then execute them.

I felt the blood drain from my face. Natasha. I had to warn Natasha.

Fredricks got up and came to my side. "Are you quite alright?" He knelt next to my chair.

I bit my lip. No, nothing was alright. Everything was wrong. Quite wrong.

He took my hand. "I won't let anything happen to you, ma chérie." He kissed my hand and then gazed into my eyes. I resisted the urge to reach out and touch his cheek. "We'll get out of this mess." He squeezed my hand.

"I just want to go home." I folded in on myself.

"And marry your young lieutenant?" Behind his smile, there was sadness in his eyes.

"Maybe." After all, no one else had proposed.

"In that case, I suppose we have to get him out of the country, too." He stood up. "Your double-crossing countryman almost got your good lieutenant killed."

"The mole." I sipped my drink.

"Indeed." Fredricks went back to the sideboard and refilled his glass.

"Did he kill Victor?"

"No." He returned with his brandy and a packet of biscuits. He offered me one.

"Who did?" I took a biscuit. "And who's the mole? Do you know?"

"I have my suspicions." He sat the packet on the table next to me. "I wish I could offer you something more substantial."

"Who?" I took a nibble of the biscuit. "Who do you suspect?"

"You won't like my answer—"

A pounding on the door interrupted him. A loud voice shouted something in Russian.

"Bloody hell." Fredricks bounded into action. "The Cheka." He grabbed my arm and pulled me off the chair. "We've got to go."

"Where?" I glanced around the suite. There was no escape. "Out the window?" We were on the third floor, for heaven's sake.

"Precisely." He dashed to the closet, opened a case, and pulled out a long rope ladder. The thing seemed to go on forever.

What in the world?

He reared back and with the heel of his boot kicked out the only intact window. He ran to the divan and pushed it against the window. With a grunt, he lifted one corner and slid the end of the ladder under the foot. "Let's go." He pulled me toward the window.

"Fredricks." My mind raced. Would we both go to jail? Would I ever see him again? Would the Cheka break through that door and shoot us on the spot? I threw my arms around his neck and kissed him.

"*Je t'aime*," he whispered into my neck. "Your beard tickles."

I laughed. He kissed me hard on the lips. The passion of his response left me breathless. I kissed him again.

The jangling of keys. The door opened. The porter stood gaping at us. Behind him, two men in black stared over his shoulders.

Fredricks lifted me onto the divan. "Go!"

Clearly flustered, the porter shut the door.

I jumped off the divan and ran to the door.

"What are you doing?" Fredricks came after me.

I grabbed my coat and hat and Kitty's forensics case.

"We don't have time." Fredricks took the case from my hands.

"I need it." I tried to grab it back, but he was too quick. "To prove my innocence."

"Fine." He dashed back to the window. "Come on, then."

I slouched into my coat and tugged on my hat and then followed his lead.

"Hurry!" Still carrying my case, Fredricks jumped up on the divan and then helped me up and onto the ladder. "Fast as you can. Don't look down."

Putting one foot after the other, I tried not to look down.

"Concentrate on the rung in front of you." Fredricks was right above me. "Faster."

Shouting from the suite signaled the Cheka's advance. We were halfway down the ladder when the shooting began. My heart raced and I quickened my pace. Shots echoed through the alley. Fredricks's boots were touching my head. My foot slipped and I was dangling from one rung. Clinging onto the rope, I regained my footing. The cold made it hard to hold on. My fingers were stiff and my eyes watered. The frigid air stung my throat. And yet I was sweating. *Concentrate on the rung in front of you.* I repeated Fredricks's directive over and over in my mind.

The ladder ended a good six feet from the ground. I closed my eyes and let go. I landed in a snowbank. Fredricks dropped the case and then let go and landed nearby. He jumped up and stomped through the snow. He helped me up. "We have to separate." He lifted me over the berm and handed me the case. "Get back to the consulate. You'll be safe there... for now." He led me to the corner and then put his fingers to his lips and whistled. The sound so close to my ear startled me and I jumped back.

A taxicab stopped. Fredricks opened the door. I stood blinking at him. He gently placed his hand on my cheek. His panther ring was cold against my skin. He kissed my forehead, and as he did, he pushed me into the cab. He shouted something to the driver in Russian and then shut the car door. From the car window, I watched as he ran up the street and disappeared around the corner.

19

FORENSICS

By the time I got back to the consulate, the sun had set. Breathless, I climbed the stairs. Clifford and Kitty were playing cards. Poppy was sleeping in Clifford's lap. Clifford and his pipe. Kitty and her strangled cursing when she lost. It was a cozy little scene. A nice antidote to nearly being hauled off to jail.

"There you are, Aunt Fiona." Kitty threw her cards in the middle of the table. "I've been waiting for you to get back with my forensics case." She stood blinking for a minute and then burst out laughing. "A family of dunnocks could live in that bloody beard."

"Yes, well. It worked." At least it worked on the parlor maid, if not Anna and Fredricks. I returned her case. "I've collected some very interesting specimens. Did you test those cigars?" I debated telling her what had happened with Fredricks but thought better of it. She didn't approve of me fraternizing with the enemy.

"How could I?" She pointed at the case. "You had my chemicals."

"Oh." I laid the case on the table. "Sorry." I wondered if the Cheka had caught up to Fredricks. Or had he got clean away?

"Toxins that kill a man instantly, you say?" She opened the case and took out two vials.

"I was in the room when he died." I nodded. "Whatever killed him was fast acting." Unless, of course, it was administered when the stranger first arrived. The mystery man had been there for hours. My poor legs still hadn't recovered from being folded like a flag under that desk. "Or fast enough to kill within seven hours." I tried to slow my racing thoughts and concentrate on the matter at hand. The cigars. Just looking at the wretched things brought back the memory of sickening cigar smoke and my hours under that awful desk.

"Instantly or seven hours?" She arched her brows. "Big difference when it comes to poisons."

"Maybe start with the quickest and simplest tests first and work our way up?" I suggested. Seemed the logical way to proceed. Although, as Fredricks had once said, "The easiest way is not always the right way."

"Right." Kitty pulled my envelope from her beaded handbag and dumped the cigar butts onto the table. Then she set to work arranging slides and test tubes. She snapped on rubber gloves and then took one of the cigar butts between her fingers. Rubbing it, she sprinkled bits onto a bead of solution she'd dropped onto a slide. "First off, I don't need a microscope to tell you this cigar contains something other than tobacco. See?" She pointed to some crumbs that had spilled onto the table. "There are yellow bits mixed with the brown."

"What is it?" I moved closer for a better look. A hint of jasmine floated in the air. The same scent I'd smelled in Victor's library.

"Uncle Clifford, would you be a dear and fetch the small brown case from the coat closet?" She batted her eyelashes. Her ridiculous schoolgirl act. She had Uncle Clifford wrapped around her little finger. He was almost as fond of her as he was her dog.

"Righto." He jumped up and dashed to the closet.

Kitty sandwiched the tobacco solution between two slides. And when Clifford delivered her case, she opened it and removed the microscope. Once the equipment was stable, she carefully slipped the slide under the lens. "Let's see." She leaned into the eyepiece. "I'm no botanist, but my best guess is gelsemium." Actually, she was an expert botanist when it came to poisons. She'd taken an entire course on the subject at her boarding school in France.

"What's gelsemium?" I removed the envelope containing the carpet fibers. Perhaps it would confirm her hypothesis.

"Heartbreak grass." She stood up. "Deadly, especially if inhaled."

"Good lord." Clifford peered into the microscope. "He was poisoned?"

"I think we've found our murder weapon." Heartbreak grass. That was a new one. But appropriate to my entire misadventure in Russia. "Is the second butt contaminated, too?"

While Clifford and I watched, she performed the same procedure on the second cigar butt. "Nope. No signs of poison."

"Unless you count tobacco." I certainly did.

Clifford removed his pipe from his mouth.

The killer must have made sure he smoked an untainted cigar and given the heartbreak grass-laced one to Iron Victor. "Where does this grass grow?" I took my turn looking into the microscope. All I saw were squiggly lines and strange cell-like circles.

"It's actually a climbing vine with beautiful, fragrant yellow flowers." Kitty removed the slide and put her microscope back in its brown case. "It grows all over India and Asia and probably in the warmer areas of Russia, too."

"Fragrant." I bent down and sniffed. "Like jasmine?" The perfume I'd smelled near Victor's body wasn't from a person. It was from the heartbreak grass in his cigar.

"Similar, yes." She closed the microscope case.

I handed her the envelope. "I collected carpet fibers in case that helps."

"We already know where he was killed." She took the envelope, dumped the contents onto a slide, and examined it. "Since he inhaled the poison, it won't show up on the carpet. But I would suggest Mrs. Volodarsky get a better housekeeper." She looked up and grinned.

I shook my head. "We know *what* killed Iron Victor. Now we just have to figure out who gave him that cigar." I unwrapped the whiskey glass. "Can you dust for fingerprints and determine who used this glass?" It may have been used by the mystery man, Anna's man-lady or the bear. Who was the fifth visitor?

"I can dust for prints." She used the cloth to pick up the glass. "But without a set to compare them to, it won't do us any good. Have anyone in mind?"

"The mole ratting on Operation Ambassadors." I paced the room to help me think. "I heard him. But was he also the killer?" I stopped at the window and looked out. It had started to snow. "Can you compare the fingerprints on the glass to prints here in this room?" I turned back to Kitty. "The mole has to be one of the ambassadors."

"But which one?" Kitty sat the glass on the table. "Unless I take their fingerprints, we won't know whose is whose."

"I say." Clifford tamped more tobacco into his pipe. "Are you absolutely sure one of our chaps sabotaged the plan?"

"It had to be one of ours." I took up pacing again. "Who else knew about the plan?" I wished Fredricks hadn't been so coy. He knew more than he was letting on. And what did he mean, I wouldn't like it?

"I don't think we'll be getting any prints. Lockhart is in custody." Kitty took out dusting powders from her case. "Archie is in hospital. And Reilly and Savinkov flew the coop. What's this?" She dumped the cuff-link out of the glass and onto the table. It clattered and spun to a stop. She picked it up and examined it. "Where did you get it?" Her voice was hard.

"I found it under the sofa in Victor's library." I took it from her. "Do you recognize it?"

"You bet your boots I do." Her eyes flashed. "Sidney Reilly." She exhaled his name.

Oh, my word. "Mr. Reilly is our mole." Somewhat circumstantial evidence. But good enough for me.

"He ratted us out to the Cheka." Kitty kicked at the chair. "I knew there was something about him I didn't like."

"And now he's flown the coop." I reached into the forensics case.

"I say." Clifford held up his pipe. "And when those other fellows were caught, he escaped."

"Bingo." I removed the phonograph record and unwrapped it.

"A record." Clifford smiled. "You know, we used to listen to that Harry Champion chap at the Turf Club. 'A Little Bit of Cucumber' and all that. I remember once, Old Smokey, that's what the fellows called him, anyway, Old Smokey took to dancing." He chuckled. "And then Barney. That's Barney Smith of Winchester—"

I held up my hand and cut him off. "Iron Victor was playing this when he died." Careful not to smudge it with my own fingerprints, I held it up by its edges. "Know anyone with a phonograph?"

"What about your new countess friend?" Kitty raised her eyebrows. "Aren't you best pals now?"

She was right. Surely the countess had access to a phonograph. If only I had access to her. I needed to find her anyway and warn her about the White Rose Directive. If she had a phonograph, then the visit could do double duty. "But where to find her?" For all I knew, she'd been exiled to Siberia with her husband... or hauled before a firing squad. "I have another reason to find her as soon as possible."

"According to the papers, she's in the penthouse at the Savoy." Clifford lit a match and held it to the bowl of his pipe.

"The Savoy." I waved away the plume of smoke. "At least the society pages are good for something." Next stop, the Savoy... with one detour.

* * *

After a detour to Novodevichy Convent, I arrived at the Savoy Hotel. Natasha was indeed staying in the penthouse. She almost slammed the door in my bearded face until I revealed my true identity. I was glad Clifford and Kitty agreed to let me go alone. The countess was as highly strung as a cat on a high wire.

A small boy held her hand. She introduced him as her son, George. Although she acted happy to see me, she was distracted and kept jumping up to sort something for George. "We're preparing him for the trip to Denmark."

"Denmark?" Every time she jumped up, I did too. "You're going to Denmark?"

She shook her head. "No. George and his nanny are going. Excuse me a moment." She disappeared into the bedroom. A few minutes later, she was back. "Apologies, but we have to get him out of the country." She paced around the sitting area, wringing her hands. "What will become of Michael?" Her round eyes filled with terror and rage—and something softer... sorrow.

I took a deep breath. *How do you go about telling someone that their whole family is targeted for execution?* "I've discovered a secret Bolshevik plot." I fiddled with the cuff of my sleeve. "Have you ever heard of the White Rose Directive?"

She shook her head.

Sigh. "I'm sorry to tell you that the Bolsheviks mean to execute the tsar and his entire family." I grimaced.

"Michael." Her lip trembled. "I hoped the rumors of his escape were true." Tears ran down her face. "But I know better."

A knock at the door startled her and she jumped. Her hand flew to her mouth. She looked at me with terror in her eyes. I didn't blame her for being jumpy.

"Let me answer it." I hoped to heaven Happy had got my message and it was her and not the secret police. I went to the door and opened it.

"Twig, is that you?" Happy took a step back. "With beard you look like Rasputin." She laughed and threw her arms around me. "Glad to see you."

"I'm glad to see you too." I nodded to the other women.

Happy had brought at least a dozen members of the Women's Battalion of Death. "Where is countess?" Happy looked over my shoulder. "Is she alright?"

"She's here." I led the women into the penthouse suite.

When she saw the countess, Happy called her troops to order. They all stood at attention. "Here to protect you, your grace." Happy gave a crisp salute. "Bolsheviks not harm hair in your head or we smash them like bug." She ground her fist into the palm of her hand. "They tough, but we more tough."

The countess gave a nervous laugh, dried her eyes, and greeted Happy with both arms extended. "Thank you, everyone." She took Happy's hands and squeezed. "You are lifesavers."

I hoped she was right.

"We stand all night in freezing cold and not complain." Happy puffed out her chest. "Happy not complain."

I hated to interrupt the reunion. So, I waited another beat and then gave a little cough. "I'm so sorry to bother you." I pulled the phonograph record from Kitty's forensics case. "Is there perhaps a phonograph here that I might use?"

The countess gave me a queer look. "You want to play a record?" As she said it, her head twitched.

"It will just take a minute." I gave her an apologetic smile. "I don't need to listen to the whole thing." I realized she wouldn't be sympathetic to my quest to find Iron Victor's killer. For all I knew, she *was* the killer. Under other circumstances, I would question her. But she was so distraught, and with the Women's Battalion of Death at her side, I didn't dare. "The Cheka think I killed Iron Victor."

She winced when I mentioned the Cheka.

"You killed Iron Victor?" Happy slapped me on the shoulder so hard I nearly fell over.

"No. I did not." I took a few steps out of her reach. "I'm trying to clear my name." I unwrapped the record.

A look of confusion on her face, the countess squinted at me. "A phonograph recording will clear your name?"

"I don't know." I had to hear what was on that record. "But I have to find out."

The countess turned to Happy. "Excuse me a minute." She put a slender hand on Happy's arm. Then she led me to a cabinet near the fireplace. "Help yourself." She made to go and then stopped and turned back. She stood looking at me but said nothing.

"Can I ask you something?" My voice was almost a whisper.

She shrugged. The gesture of a woman defeated.

"Do you know anything about Iron Victor's murder?" I opened the cabinet and then twisted around to watch her reaction.

She flushed. "All I know is I'm glad the *pridurki* is dead."

"Did you kill him?" There, I'd said it.

"Are you mad?" She laughed. "You can't believe..." Her laughter became hysterical. With the backs of her hands, she wiped away tears from her eyes. Her head jerked again. A nervous twitch?

"I'm sorry." The way she laughed made me afraid. "I didn't mean to..."

She cleared her throat and straightened to her full height, which was considerably shorter than me. "I only wish I had." With that, she left me and rejoined the Women's Battalion of Death.

I gave a sigh of relief. No one confessed to a murder with the words "I only wish I had." No. The countess did not kill Victor. Thank goodness.

I cranked the machine and then lifted the phonograph arm and put it to the record. After a few seconds of static crackles, a man's voice boomed to life. Vladimir Lenin shouting in Russian. *V. Lenin's Speeches 1917.* I recognized the voice. It was the same voice I'd heard shouting in Iron Victor's library the night he was killed. And I was pretty sure the words Lenin was barking were the exact same ones I'd heard that night from under the desk. "The fatherland is in danger... Defend the fatherland."

Good heavens. It wasn't the mystery man delivering a speech to Victor. It was a recording of Lenin. That meant the murder could have taken place much earlier than I thought it had. The killer must have put on the record to cover his tracks. I racked my brain. What was the last thing I'd heard before Lenin's speech? When was the last time I'd heard Victor speak? Who was still in the room with Victor when he died? And how long was I under that blooming desk listening to records?

20

HEARTBREAK GRASS

After my visit to the countess, I returned to the consulate. That night, I slept there on a folding cot. Kitty and I slept in one room. Clifford slept in the living room. The next morning, I rose early and paced the floors like a caged tiger. How much longer could I hide out in the consulate? Eventually, the Cheka would disregard diplomacy and arrest me. Waiting was killing me. My friends, on the other hand, appeared unusually relaxed. With his long legs stretched out, Clifford sat in front of the fireplace reading a newspaper. Probably the social pages. Kitty was reading a fashion magazine. If you could call that "reading."

I'd tried to settle into a chair with a book I'd found on a small shelf in the front room. A detective story called *The Red Thumb Mark*. Dr. John Thorndyke was no Sherlock Holmes, but he was a jolly clever detective, nonetheless. His prowess with forensics put me in mind of Kitty with her test tubes and microscope. When I got to the part where Dr. Thorndyke received a poisoned cigar, I began to suspect the coincidence of the book at the consulate was no coincidence at all.

Yes. It made no sense that Sidney Reilly told Iron Victor about

Operation Ambassadors and then killed him. But when did murder ever make sense? I couldn't just sit here and wait for the police to haul me in. I put the book down and circled the room again.

"Quit pacing." Kitty peered over the edge of her magazine. "You're making me nervous."

She should be nervous. I was nervous. The Cheka could show up at any minute and cart me off. I wasn't any closer to discovering who killed Iron Victor. Except I knew how they'd killed him. And we strongly suspected Sidney Reilly was the mole. I jammed my hands in the pockets of my skirt. The bloody photograph. The one Archie clutched in his hand. The photograph of me. Who gave Archie this photograph of me in front of the Metropol Hotel? Had Sidney Reilly delivered the file on me and the other women who'd escaped and then taken my picture with him? Why? To give it to Archie? Again, why? Or had Iron Victor's killer taken the picture? It had to have been someone who was in the library with Victor the night he was killed.

After another thirty minutes of pacing, I resolved to visit Archie. From all reports, he was going to make a full recovery. But I wanted to see for myself. Plus, I needed to ask him where he got that photograph. I stopped in the middle of the room and announced, "I'm going to the clinic."

"You can't go out." Kitty shook her finger at me. "Not unless you want to end up back in jail."

Unfortunately, she was right. "I can't, but Sir Edward Burnett Tylor can." I gave her a sly smile.

"You and your get-ups." Now she sounded like Captain Hall. She cooed at the little dog on her lap. "Aunt Fiona's beard will never be as fine as yours, Poppy-poo." The pup licked her chin.

Disgusting.

I retired to the lavatory with my mustache case and Sir

Edward Burnett Tylor's woolen trousers and starched white shirt. As I applied the mustache and beard, the smell of spirit glue cheered me considerably. My poor skin wasn't as pleased. Still red from the last application—and even worse the removal—it stung.

"Are you sure about this?" Kitty asked when I emerged from the bathroom. "It's risky."

"Would you like company?" Clifford glanced up from his newspaper.

"No." I realized I'd said it a bit too abruptly. "But thank you, dear Clifford." I didn't need a chaperone. And even less a blabbermouth.

* * *

When I got to the clinic, Archie was sitting up in bed, which I took to be a good sign. He stared at me with an odd look on his face. I stood gazing at him, a big smile on my face. Thank goodness he was going to be alright.

"Have we met?" He narrowed his brows and squinted at me. "You look familiar, but I'm afraid I'm not quite myself yet."

"I'm not quite myself, either." I grinned.

"Fiona." His shoulders shook with laughter. "Is that you under that beast of a beard?" Gasping, he held his side where it was bandaged. "Ouch. Don't make me laugh."

"I didn't dare come as myself." I pulled up a chair. "But I had to see you."

"I'm so glad you're here." He reached out to take my hand and then thought better of it. "You're quite the girl."

"At this moment, most would disagree." I winked. "At least I hope so."

"You saved my life." He blushed. "And I think it only proper that I devote the rest of it to making you happy."

I thought of Fredricks and his pig satisfied. "Seeing you on the mend is all I need."

"You know what I mean." His cheeks darkened even more.

"Can you stop this bloody war?" That would make me happy. Fredricks claimed he could... with my help. Bloody ridiculous.

"We'll beat them. You'll see." He gave me a weak smile. "We can't quit living just because the Jerrys are trying to kill us. Otherwise, they've already won."

We were trying to kill them too. Still, he had a point. Watching him almost die had been too much for me. I couldn't go through that again. And yet I'd promised. I'd promised if Archie survived then I'd marry him. "I don't want to lose you."

"So, let's get married." He grabbed my hand. "Let's do it now. I don't want to wait." His voice was eager and hopeful. How could I let him down?

"We should at least wait until I'm not wearing trousers and a beard."

"True." He laughed again. "I prefer my beautiful bride in a wedding gown."

"And I prefer my handsome groom standing at an altar." I lifted his hand to my lips and kissed it. A groan from the next cot reminded me I was in a public place. Not only that, but I was also dressed as a man. If the Cheka didn't arrest me for murder, they just might arrest me for indecency. Let them! I held his hand.

"Just as soon as we're back in London." His voice was full of excitement. "You pick the altar and I'll be there."

"Deal." I shook his hand. I had made a deal. A deal with heaven. I couldn't go back on it now. And I wanted to marry him. Right? I loved him. Didn't I? Then why did I have this uncanny niggling at the back of my mind? I pushed it away. "As soon as we're back in London."

His face radiated happiness. "I can get through anything with you by my side, sweet Fiona."

I reached out and brushed the hair from his forehead. My beloved unruly lock.

"Darling, would you fetch my cigarettes?" He smiled.

I bit my tongue. I hated those foul Kenilworths. But how could I resist that smile? I'd work on weaning him off cigarettes after we were married. "Where are they?" I thought of Sherlock Holmes, who kept his tobacco in the toe end of a Persian slipper.

"In my jacket pocket." He pointed to a closet near the entrance. "An orderly brought me one yesterday. Don't know why he didn't just bring the whole damn pack." He shook his head. "The strangest thing. Tragic, really."

"What?" The way his countenance had clouded over made me worried.

"Today he's dead." He sighed. "Died last night while having a smoke behind the clinic. You just never know how long you've got." His face brightened again. "That's why we've got to make the most of it and get married now... you and me, my darling Fiona."

"And we will." I nodded. "We'll be smashing." I went to the closet and thumbed through the hangers until I found Archie's jacket. I recognized the fabric despite the tremendous dark bloodstains. "Which pocket?" I called across the room.

"Inside breast pocket."

I slipped my hand into the pocket and pulled out the pack of Kenilworths. As I did, my fingers brushed against a cigarette case. Odd. Why did he have a packet of cigarettes *and* a cigarette case? Maybe the case was empty, or he hadn't filled it yet. The case was silver with a tree etched on its face. I turned it over and appreciated the weight of it in my palm and then opened it. Maybe Archie would like me to fill it for him.

Oh, my sainted aunt. Inside the case lay a single cigar. Its label sported the popular comic figure, Punch. A cigar exactly like the one that had been used to poison Iron Victor. My mind was awhirl. Anna's man-lady. I glanced over at Archie's beautiful face. The photograph in Archie's hand as he lay dying. Torn from the file in Victor's library the night Victor was killed. Archie's delirious words: "Punch... Fiona." Had he been trying to tell me about the Punch cigar? I felt like I'd swallowed a rock. Make that a landslide.

It took a full minute to catch my breath before I went back to Archie's cot. I held out the case. "Is this what you wanted?"

His eyes went wide, and he snatched the case from my hand. "Where did you get that?"

"From your pocket." Where did he think I'd got it? I didn't exactly go rummaging to find it. It was right there along with his Kenilworths. Had he forgotten about it? Or had someone planted it there? I hoped to heaven someone had. Otherwise, I'd found Iron Victor's killer. I was looking right at him.

"Which pocket?" His accusatory tone stung worse than the spirit glue.

"Inside breast pocket. Just like you said." I produced the packet of cigarettes and handed it to him.

He took the pack and tapped out a cigarette. Then he reached inside the pack and retrieved a small box of matches. His hands trembled. Holding the cigarette between his lips, he struck the match and lit it. After a long drag, he blew out a cloud of smoke. Without a word, he looked over at me and then opened the case. "Good God." He glanced around wildly. "There's one missing."

Now I was really confused. Had someone stolen one of Archie's poisoned cigars and used it to kill Iron Victor? More to the point, why did Archie have poisoned cigars? "What do you mean?" I stared down at him, wondering if I really knew him.

"I had two left. This case was in the pocket of my overcoat and not my jacket. Someone took a cigar and moved the case." He was breathless.

"So what?" Why did it matter which pocket it was in? Unless he didn't want me to find it.

"The orderly." He ran his hand through his hair. "Dear God." The blood drained from his face. "Go out behind the clinic and see if you find part of a cigar just like this one." He held out the case. "Wear gloves to pick it up." His tone was hard.

"Why?" I knew why. It was poisoned too. The unsuspecting orderly must have thought he'd found a nice treat, taken it outside to enjoy it, and bam. He fell dead. Just like Iron Victor. "Don't tell me. Gelsemium."

"How did you know?" He gripped the edge of his blanket. "Heartbreak grass."

Heartbreak grass, indeed. I met his gaze. "Why did you kill him?"

"Orders." He sighed. "That and he'd discovered your cover. He would have had you executed."

I dropped into the chair next to his cot. Archie had killed Iron Victor. He did it for me? I knew he was an assassin for the War Office, but still... "You took the photograph from the file. You were there." How did I not know? I would have recognized his voice whatever language he spoke. I should have sensed his presence. Curses. He came when I'd fallen asleep on the job. That was the only explanation.

He beckoned me closer, and I leaned in. "Victor knew about Operation Ambassadors." His voice was raspy. "I was under orders to take out Victor before he informed his men." He shook his head. "Headquarters thinks we could have a mole." He fell back against his pillow. "The whole thing was a total cock-up."

"Victor must have told his men and they set a trap." I sucked in air. "Thank heavens you survived." I didn't tell him our suspicions about Reilly. I wanted to report it myself. Another offering to Captain Hall in hopes of forgiveness.

"Thanks to you, I survived." He leaned forward and took my hand. "I'm so sorry you're mixed up in this mess. I never meant for you to take the blame. I never meant to put you in danger." His voice broke.

"I know." I squeezed his hand. Working undercover was a dangerous business. I knew that when I'd signed on. What if I hadn't found the cigars? What if I never discovered that Archie was the assassin? Was he going to let me take the rap? No. Archie wouldn't do that.

"You need to leave." Archie's countenance hardened.

"Why?" Was he angry that I'd discovered he was the killer?

"You need to get out of Russia." There was panic in his voice. "Get out while you can... before it's too late."

"What about you?" It was only a matter of time before the Cheka figured out who really killed Iron Victor. Once they discovered what killed the orderly and where he got the tainted cigar, they'd put two and two together and know it was Archie.

"Don't worry about me." He ran his hand through his hair again. "I'll be fine." He gave me a weak smile. "I'll see you back in London and we can make plans."

"Plans?" I squinted at him. What plans?

"Wedding plans." His smile brightened.

I nodded. "Oh, right." How could he think about wedding plans? He'd just admitted to murder. Not just one, but two, if you count the poor orderly.

"Go now." He pressed his palms together. "And, darling, could you do me a favor?"

"Anything." I forced a smile.

"Collect the poisoned cigar butt from the alley." He said it matter-of-factly, as if he was asking me to fetch his hat or slippers. "We don't need the Cheka finding the evidence."

The evidence he'd killed an innocent man by accident. "Alright."

"Good girl." He beamed.

KITTY'S INTERLUDE
12 MARCH, 6 P.M.

Bang. Bang.

The pounding on the door started Poppy barking and interrupted Kitty and Clifford's card game. Kitty answered the door. Too bad. She was winning.

"What's wrong?" Kitty pulled her friend inside.

"The Cheka know everything." Olga was breathless. "You've got to get out now." She handed Kitty a large envelope. "Here. Take this."

"What is it?" Kitty danced around Poppy as the pup ran circles around her legs.

"Papers and fake passports." Olga glanced around. "Where's Figg?"

"She insisted on visiting Archie at the clinic." Kitty scooped up Poppy. "Why?"

Clifford joined them at the door. "I say, what's going on?"

"The Cheka is coming for her," Olga panted. "You've got to leave now." She thrust a paper sack at Kitty. "Your disguises." She pulled on Kitty's sleeve. "Come on. They'll be here any minute."

"Good lord." Clifford stood blinking.

"Let me grab my forensics case." Kitty rushed to the table and grabbed her case. She sat the dog and the case down only long enough to throw on her coat. "Uncle Clifford, go get the consulate car." She snatched a set of keys from a hook by the door and tossed them to him. "Catch."

The ambassadors were either in jail or had flown the coop. They wouldn't miss their car.

21

THE AINSWORTHS

The alley behind the clinic was dark and cold. In the moonlight, I could see my breath. At least the dry, freezing air made the smells of horse manure and vegetable rot sharper but less nauseating. I pulled my torch from my coat pocket and shone the beam on the ground next to the back door. There were cigarette butts everywhere. Obviously, the orderly had been using this spot to smoke on a regular basis. Squatting, I used my pencil to sift through the butts. Disgusting. A glint caught my eye. I focused the beam on it and then poked at it with the tip of my pencil. A cigar butt, complete with band. With a gloved hand, I pinched it between my thumb and forefinger. I held it up like a dirty rag. Sure enough, I was greeted by that uncanny grin. Punch the clown. I'd found the culprit. I wrapped the butt in my handkerchief and tucked it into my coat pocket.

Sounds of footfalls stopped me in my tracks. My pulse quickened. The sounds were approaching fast and from two directions. I swung around. Three men dressed in black were barely visible. Guns drawn, they rushed at me, shouting in Russian. I threw my

hands in the air. "Don't shoot. I'm unarmed." I remembered my
disguise. Crikey. To them, I looked like a strange man rummaging
around in an alley.

Two men in uniforms approached from the other end of the
alley. I was surrounded. My heart was racing. Hands still in the
air, I yelled, "I'm unarmed. Don't shoot." How the heck did you
say don't shoot in Russian? I racked my brain for the words. "*Ne
strelyay!*" I hoped I'd said don't shoot.

"You're under arrest for the murder of Chief Victor Volodarsky." One of the uniformed men pointed his gun in my face. At
least he spoke English.

"You've got it all wrong." I couldn't tell them who really killed
Iron Victor. In that hospital bed, Archie was a sitting duck. "He
was already dead when I found him."

"Tell that to the chief." The officer grabbed my arm.

I glanced up and down the alley. Could I make a run for it? I
shuddered. It was no use. They'd got me. Now I was going to
spend the rest of my life in a stinking Russian jail. Or worse. Actually, nothing could be worse. Even a firing squad would be better
than going back to that foul place.

Whiz. A black boot came out of the darkness and smacked
into the side of the officer's head. The copper dropped like a sack
of potatoes. Two whirling boots, one after the other, slammed
into one face and then the other. More coppers down.

"Aunt Fiona," Kitty shouted in my direction. "Get down!"

The remaining two Cheka fired their guns. I hit the ground.
The impact knocked the wind out of me. With another butterfly
kick, Kitty dropped them both. I patted my arms and then my
legs. Had I been hit? I hurt all over. I seemed to be in one piece.
Which was more than I could say for the Cheka. The ones who
were still conscious moaned. One was bleeding profusely from

his nose, which was most certainly broken. The face of another looked cockeyed, most likely because his jaw was broken.

"Are you alright?" Kitty held out her hand and I took it. With one graceful move, she hauled me upright. "Hop it. Those coppers won't be down forever."

I brushed off my trousers. "Let me catch my breath."

Kitty tugged at my sleeve. "We've got to go." She took off into the night like a brown hare. I tried to keep up. I stumbled over some unidentified lump in the alley. I didn't need any more obstacles. I was quite capable of tripping over my own feet—especially when they were in men's size ten shoes.

I burst out of the alley and glanced both ways. Where had she gone?

"Over here," she shouted.

I followed her voice around the corner. I found her standing next to an idling motorcar. The forest-green Vauxhall. I recognized it from the consulate.

"Get in," she barked, and then hopped in the backseat. Ecstatic to see her mistress, Poppy turned circles on the seat.

I slid into the passenger's seat.

"Hit it!" Kitty's high voice exploded right into my ear. Did she really need to yell? Poppy barked. They made an awful noise for two small creatures.

"Gladly." Clifford stomped on the accelerator and the motorcar lurched forward.

I'd barely had time to slam my door shut before we took off into the darkness. "Where are we going?" I held onto the seat for dear life.

The car rounded the corner and skidded to a stop in front of the clinic.

"To save your fiancé." Kitty opened the car door. "Anything to stop you flirting with Fredricks," she said under her breath on her way out.

"Be right back, old thing." Clifford bounded out of the car after her.

A minute later, they returned with Archie propped up between them and pulled him along. He had his arms around their shoulders. They had their arms around his waist. Kitty opened the back seat and Archie collapsed into the car. Panting, he swung his legs inside. Kitty slammed the door and then ran around the car and jumped in the back seat with him. Clifford resumed his place behind the wheel.

"Everyone ready to leg it?" Clifford's voice was full of excitement. He was obviously having the time of his life. He glanced over and flashed a smile.

The jolt of the car's acceleration threw me forward. I caught myself against the dashboard. I knew better than to criticize his driving while we were making our get-away. But really, couldn't he be more careful?

"Where are we going?" I dug my nails into the seat.

"Home!" Kitty said it more like a command than an answer.

I twisted around. What in the world? She was changing clothes in the back seat of the car. Really. What would she do next? There were men present. Although Archie was in no condition to appreciate her fine figure. Curled up in a ball, he grimaced and sucked air.

"What are you doing?" I glared at her.

"What does it look like?" She glared back.

"Don't get shirty with me, young lady," I scolded her.

Poppy bared her teeth and growled at me. "Not you, Poppy-poo."

Kitty changed out of her all-black fencing outfit into a frilly striped pinafore that made her look twelve.

"You're not really my aunt, you know." She thrust a paper sack at me. "Put this on."

I sat blinking at her.

"Take it." She shoved it in my direction.

I took the bag and opened it. A gray wig. A huge ugly skirt. Wire eyeglasses. And a knitted shawl.

"Put them on," Kitty barked.

"You don't need to shout." Her agitation was contagious. I was quite on edge.

"Hurry up." She waved her arms at me as if conducting an orchestra.

I knew better than to question Kitty when she was barking orders. I did as I was told. I yanked off my wig and ripped off my mustache. Ouch. Then I wriggled the extra-large skirt over my trousers and tugged on the gray chignon. I wrapped the wire frames around my ears and the shawl around my shoulders. "Satisfied?"

She nodded and held out a folded letter and a passport. "Your papers."

I took them and opened the passport. I was traveling as Mrs. Ainsworth. Was there a Mr. Ainsworth? I glanced back at Archie. Kitty helped him sit up and then brushed the hair out of his eyes. She pulled her forensics case off the floor and opened it. She tapped two small pills out of a tube. "Take these. They'll help with the pain."

He popped them into his mouth.

Kitty produced a newsboy cap and clapped it over Archie's hair. It made his lovely face look even more boyish.

"What's our cover story?" I tucked the false papers into my jacket pocket.

"You're Mrs. Ainsworth and Clifford is Mr. Ainsworth, and Archie and I are your adult children."

I scoffed. Why did I have to be the old lady? Who would believe I was their mother? She was a mere seven years younger than me and Archie was actually a year older. It was absurd. And Clifford as my husband? *Sigh*. Not again.

"I say, old bean." Clifford chuckled. "I made an honest woman out of you, even if you've made me old before my time."

I gave him the evil eye. Honest woman, my white knuckles.

Would the border patrol believe we were a family of four? "And what is this little family doing escaping Russia in a British diplomat's car?"

"We're not escaping." Kitty leaned against Archie's shoulder to keep him upright. "We're going back home to attend your older daughter's wedding."

"Older daughter!" How old was this Mrs. Ainsworth anyway? "Should I paint wrinkles around my eyes?"

"That's why you have glasses." She snorted. "Haven't you always wanted to be an old married lady with children?"

I huffed. What I wanted was irrelevant. My body had other ideas. "I'm not that old." I thought of one of my grandmother's sayings: Old enough to know better and young enough not to care. I was neither.

As we reached the city limits, the car slowed to a stop at the first checkpoint. Clifford rolled down the window and presented our papers. "I say, fine weather for March." He chatted up the guard. "I remember one March, when I was in India, on a hunting trip in the Himalayas." He chuckled. "We'd barely gained five hundred feet elevation when a blizzard hit." He kept up the chatter nonstop while the guard examined each passport in turn, looking from each of us back to our photographs.

"It was the damnedest thing." Clifford smiled. "Our tent collapsed, and we were buried under a foot of snow." He laughed. "And you'll never guess what happened."

"Pass, please." The guard handed back our papers and waved us through. No doubt he was tired of Clifford's nattering on. His constant prattle was disarming, I'd give him that. Clifford could test the patience of a saint.

22

HOMECOMING

By some miracle, Clifford's easy manner and open countenance got us through several more checkpoints. We all breathed a sigh of relief when we crossed the border into Finland. We couldn't take the most direct route home because it would take us across Germany. The War Office had arranged for us to make passage on a navy ship from Norway to Britain. Thanks to the Tonnage Agreement, Norway had become a neutral ally and, unbeknownst to Germany, the British Navy controlled Norwegian merchant ships. Lucky for us.

Unlucky for me, it was a turbulent passage. I was sick most of the time in a blur of delirious nausea. The rough sea didn't affect my friends, who spent the voyage playing cards with the seamen and entertaining them with Poppy's tricks. By the time we reached Britain, Archie was quite recovered. Enough so that he helped Clifford carry me off the ship.

Kitty stayed with me at my flat for the first two days back in London. She and Poppy nursed me back to health by forcing me to drink broth and tea. By the third day, I'd regained my appetite and my land-legs and yearned for privacy and quiet. Kitty and

Poppy were dear creatures, but loud. After a particularly raucous game of fetch, my downstairs neighbor complained about the racket.

Kitty finally agreed to leave me on my own. But only if she could take me wedding shopping on Saturday. She wouldn't leave my flat until I acquiesced.

I still couldn't believe I was really engaged. Even more astounding was that the wedding date was set for 22 June, summer solstice. It had taken all my powers of persuasion to get Archie to agree to wait that long.

By Saturday, I'd regained my strength, if not my appetite for shopping. Usually, I was keen for a trip to Harrods or Liberty's, especially if it meant buying a new gown for a posh assignment. My favorite place to shop was Angel's Fancy Dress—although a wedding gown was a costume of sorts, it didn't exactly count as a disguise. And I doubted Archie would approve if I turned up at the church wearing trousers and a mustache.

Kitty was coming at ten o'clock to take me to Savile Row to get fitted for a wedding dress, and then on to Harrods to shop for honeymoon attire. Since Archie and I hadn't decided where we would go yet—or even if we could get away—I didn't know what I'd need. What climate? What activities? Ahem. I could of course anticipate certain activities that might take me to the lingerie department. My cheeks warmed.

I had two hours to get ready. Soaking in the bath, I took stock of my trip to Moscow. Life was full of surprises. I'd gone for a romantic tryst with Fredricks and returned engaged to Archie. My assignment had been to spy on Iron Victor and instead I was wanted for his murder. I'd sleuthed out the real murderer. But I couldn't tell anyone, at least not while I was still in Russia. Operation Ambassadors was a bust. I'd heard that Sidney Reilly had managed to smooth talk his way back into service. But he wasn't called the Ace of Spies for nothing. Slippery devil. Fredricks had been instrumental in the Bolsheviks signing a peace treaty with Germany. He claimed he was working for peace and not for Germany. I believed him... sort of. The War Office did not. In fact, I was to report to Captain Hall's office on Monday to debrief on everything I'd learned about Fredricks from "trailing him" to Moscow. Thanks to Kitty, as far as my boss knew, I was trailing Fredricks for duty and not desire.

Where was Fredricks now?

When I closed my eyes, I was back in his embrace. That last kiss. Before we climbed out the window. The scent of sandalwood and mustache wax. My beard entangled with his. His warm breath on my neck. *Stop it, Fiona. You're engaged to another man.* I shivered. My bath had gone cold. I stepped out of the tub and toweled off.

Kitty was right. You shouldn't separate duty and desire. It was my duty *not* to love Fredricks. He was the enemy.

And Archie? Was it my duty to love him?

I did love him. I'd better love him. I was going to marry him, after all. And if loving him coincided with my duty, so be it.

I went to my bedroom to select an appropriate outfit. Kitty had told me to dress up because she was taking me to Fortnum & Mason for a fancy tea after shopping. I was looking forward to cucumber sandwiches and a nice strong cuppa.

I chose my favorite lavender gabardine dress. It had an adorable white fur collar and matching fur around the sleeves. And I had the perfect hat to go with it. A deep purple tam with white feathers. I completed the ensemble with ivory kid gloves and an ivory beaded handbag. Tea at Fortnum & Mason was a treat and I planned to make the most of it.

A knock at the door signaled Kitty's arrival. She looked smart in a lacey pink frock and a little pink sailor's cap. Poppy wore a matching pink bow in her topknot. To my surprise, Kitty had hired a car. Unfortunately, the driver got lost and we ended up at Primrose Hill park, of all places.

"Since we're here, do you mind if we take Poppy out for a wee?" Kitty didn't wait for my answer. Instead, she opened the car door and hopped out. Tail wagging, Poppy followed her mistress.

"Oh, alright." It was a pleasant day for the end of March. The sun was high in the sky. The sky was almost blue. And blooming daffodils fashioned torrents of brilliant yellow along the garden paths. I followed Kitty and Poppy to the top of the hill. They headed for one of the benches and took a seat. I joined them. It was a lovely day to take in the view of the city below.

"Aunt Fiona, you wait here while I take Poppy for her potty break."

I nodded.

Kitty led the beastie by the leash and headed for the open grass.

I welcomed the chance to sit and relax. Out of the corner of my eye, I glimpsed a soldier in uniform coming toward me. When I turned my head, I was met with a vision that set my heart soaring. My hand flew to my mouth. Archie in full dress uniform, the sun in his chestnut hair, and a smile on his beautiful face.

He reached the bench and gazed down at me. "Darling Fiona."

"Archie, what are you doing here?" Tears welled in my eyes.

He dropped to one knee. "I want to do it properly."

My heart leaped into my throat. I felt like I might be sick.

"Fiona Figg, would you do me the honor of becoming my wife?" He held out a small velvet box and then snapped it open to reveal a gorgeous gold ring with a small diamond set in a rose-petal design. "It was my grandmother's." He plucked the ring from the box and then took my hand. Tears trickled down my cheeks as he slipped it onto my finger.

"Oh, Archie." I leaned forward to kiss him. "It's lovely."

"You're lovely." He was especially adorable when he blushed. He slid in next to me on the bench. "I have something else." He reached into his pocket and pulled out another larger jewelry box. "An engagement present. One that belongs only to you." He held it out to me.

I took it and slowly opened it. A gold heart with a zagged split down the middle. Two halves of the same heart hung on two gold chains, one thick and one fine. I glanced over at Archie. Wet with tears, his green eyes sparkled in the sunlight.

"My heart belongs only to you." He took the smaller chain from the box and held it up.

I turned and he fastened it around my neck. I touched it. Half a heart. I took the other half and fastened it around his neck. Two halves of the same heart.

"You're my best girl. A real brick." He took me in his arms. "I love you, Fiona."

"I love you, too," I whispered. Just then, a solid black cat with mischief in its eyes ran out of the bushes. It crossed behind the bench and ran up a tree. It looked like a miniature panther. The cat sat watching me from a low branch. I stuck out my tongue at it. The little panther yawned and then stretched out on the branch like it had all the time in the world.

KITTY'S EPILOGUE
23 MARCH, 11 A.M.

Kitty hid behind a tree and watched.

Poppy squirmed in her arms, but she held on tight. She didn't want the dog to get away and ruin it.

When Archie went down on one knee, she blinked away a tear.

"Finally," she whispered. Finally, Aunt Fiona would marry her flyboy. "Then she can settle down and get to work."

Kitty straightened the pup's pink bow and held her up to gaze into her big brown eyes. "You're my beloved. Always and forever."

The dog licked her face, and she couldn't help but giggle. She kissed Poppy's wet little nose and then hugged her close.

"Right, Poppy-poo?"

A NOTE FROM THE AUTHOR
FUN FACTS

Although I've taken creative liberties, many of the characters and events in this novel are based on real people and real events. Fredrick Fredricks is based on real-life spy Fritz Duquesne, the South African huntsman who spied for the Germans in both World War I and World War II. Reportedly, he escaped capture and prison several times, donned various personae, and was a real charmer.

The story is set in March 1918 when the Bolsheviks, led by Vladimir Lenin and with the help of Leon Trotsky, finalized a peace treaty with Germany and withdrew from World War I, and moved the capital from Petrograd to Moscow. They signed the treaty on 3 March, and moved on 10 March, even though they had announced the move would be one day later.

Operation Ambassadors is based on a real plot to kidnap and kill the Bolshevik leaders. The ambassadors involved were British ambassador Sir Robert Lockhart, British spy Sidney Reilly (known as the Ace of Spies and the basis for Ian Fleming's James Bond character), and Russian revolutionary Boris Savinkov. There was a fourth ambassador whom I cut out to avoid too many characters and more confusions: American ambassador DeWitt Clinton Poole. There was a mole who told the Cheka, the secret police. Some suspect it was Sidney Reilly, although that was never proven.

Iron Victor is inspired by a composite of several real-life figures who worked for the Cheka secret police: Yakov Peters (known as Peter the painter), Felix Dzerzhinsky (known as Iron Felix, once the head of the Cheka), Moisei Uritsky (assassinated August 1918, once head of the Cheka), and V. Volodarsky (assassinated 20 June 1918). Reportedly, Volodarsky's assassination was an inciting incident for the execution of the royal family.

Tsar Nicholas II and his family were exiled, moved at least twice, and executed on 16–17 July 1918. There was talk of bringing the Russian royal family to England, where Nicholas would join his cousin King George V. But the English royal family were afraid harboring the Russian royal family might incite rebellion against the monarchy at home. So, they refused to grant them asylum. Nicholas II was known for his tyrannical ruling style. This, combined with the hardships and famine resulting from World War I, led to the Russian revolution of October 1917.

The character of Maria Rada "Happy" Bochkareva is based on the real leader of the Women's Battalion of Death, Maria Bochkareva, whose autobiography *Yashka: My Life as a Peasant, Exile and Soldier* is a fascinating read. Born to a peasant family, she married young and along with her husband was a laborer in Siberia. He abused her and she fled, only to be put to work in a brothel. She formed the all-women combat unit and maintained that the women could shame the men into standing up for their country. A committed Russian nationalist, she was imprisoned by the Bolsheviks several times. Eventually, she fled to New York, where she dictated her memoir. In April 1919, she returned to

Russia. She was captured by the Cheka, interrogated for months, and then executed on 16 March 1920.

Peggy Hull is also based on a real American journalist who reported from Russia and was sympathetic to the Bolsheviks.

Countess Brasova is based on the real Natalia (Natasha), Countess Brasova, wife of the tsar's brother Michael. She did send her young son to Denmark with his nanny and eventually escaped to England. Although rumored to have escaped, Michael was executed 12–13 June 1918.

After twenty years in Germany, in December 1914, after the outbreak of war, Russian painter Wassily Kandinsky returned to Russia. He did work for the Department of Visual Arts in the People's Commissariat of Enlightenment (NARKOMPROS) and took a position as a director of the Museum of Painting and Culture in 1918. In 1921, he moved back to Berlin. The full quotation from Kandinsky is from a letter he wrote to an artist friend:

The sun melts all of Moscow down to a single spot that, like a mad tuba, starts all of the heart and all of the soul vibrating. But no, this uniformity of red is not the most beautiful hour. It is only the final chord of a symphony that takes every color to the zenith of life that, like the fortissimo of a great orchestra, is both compelled and allowed by Moscow to ring out.

ACKNOWLEDGEMENTS

As always, thanks to the Boldwood team, with special thanks to my editors, Rachel, Cecily and Susan. Thanks to my critique group—Benigno, Lorraine, Fred, and Susan—for helpful suggestions on the first chapters. I'm grateful for my family and their patience with me as I holed up like a hermit in my summer cabin in Idaho when they thought I should be on vacation. Finally, huge thanks to Beni, Mischief, Mayhem, and Mr. Flan for being there through everything.

ABOUT THE AUTHOR

Kelly Oliver is the award-winning, bestselling author of three mysteries series. She is also the Distinguished Professor of Philosophy at Vanderbilt University and lives in Nashville Tennessee.

Sign up to Kelly Oliver's mailing list here for news, competitions and updates on future books.

Visit Kelly's website: http://www.kellyoliverbooks.com/

Follow Kelly on social media:

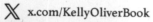

X x.com/KellyOliverBook

f facebook.com/kellyoliverauthor

instagram.com/kellyoliverbooks

tiktok.com/@kellyoliverbooks

BB bookbub.com/authors/kelly-oliver

ALSO BY KELLY OLIVER

A Fiona Figg & Kitty Lane Mystery Series

Chaos at Carnegie Hall

Covert in Cairo

Mayhem in the Mountains

Arsenic at Ascot

Murder in Moscow

Poison
& Pens

POISON & PENS IS THE HOME OF
COZY MYSTERIES SO POUR YOURSELF
A CUP OF TEA & GET SLEUTHING!

DISCOVER PAGE-TURNING NOVELS FROM
YOUR FAVOURITE AUTHORS &
MEET NEW FRIENDS

JOIN OUR
FACEBOOK GROUP

BIT.LYPOISONANDPENSFB

SIGN UP TO OUR
NEWSLETTER

BIT.LY/POISONANDPENSNEWS

Boldwood

Boldwood Books is an award-winning fiction publishing company seeking out the best stories from around the world.

Find out more at www.boldwoodbooks.com

Join our reader community for brilliant books, competitions and offers!

Follow us
@BoldwoodBooks
@TheBoldBookClub

Sign up to our weekly deals newsletter

https://bit.ly/BoldwoodBNewsletter